I0594467

The Priestess Chronicles
Volume 1

Call
of the
Druids

Books by Fiona Tarr

Covenant of Grace Series

Destiny of Kings
Seed of Hope
Legacy of Power
Heir of Vengeance
The Ehud Dagger – Novella

The Eternal Realm

The Jericho Prophecy
Delilah and the Dark God
Reign of Retribution

The Priestess Chronicles

Call of the Druids
Relic Seeker
Shiloh Rising

Chapter 1

'Come on Ariela! Focus!' Salaman swung his hefty sword around his wrist as though it were no heavier than a wooden practice sword. The muscles in his upper arms bulged with the weight, but everything about his stance spoke of balance and experience.

'I am focussed. It's this damn heat.' Ariela wiped her sweating hands on her tunic, before regaining a grip on the staff, her frustration evident in the crease of her forehead as she prepared herself for attack.

'Your enemies will not always be so kind as to afford you the perfect weather when they attack. It could be pouring with rain and you will still need to focus.' Salaman pointed his blade at the young woman and stared down the weapon accusingly.

Ariela scowled at her father. 'Why are you always such an ass when you train me and so charming with all the other Priestesses?' Ariela tried unsuccessfully to keep the whine from her words.

'Oh child, you wound me with your accusation.' Salaman mocked her with a smile before stepping in undeterred, slowly circling her. He watched Ariela warily. 'Trust your training. Trust your instincts. You are just like your mother was when I trained her, feisty but you need to focus that passion girl.'

Ariela moved forward to meet Salaman. Her weapon was smaller and lighter than her father's yet it still took great precision and power to bring it to bear. The muscles in her back rippled with each contact between the weapons as the sound rang out around the arena.

A small group of Priestesses had stopped to watch the training and looked on, pointing and chatting quietly over who might win this bout. Ariela looked up from the arena to the balcony of the nearby dormitory and frowned at the audience.

Salaman saw the distraction and moved in, raising the butt of his weapon and striking Ariela in the shoulder of her sword arm. She staggered back, losing her balance, yet smoothly recovering as she spun with the momentum, pivoting as a dancer might under different circumstances.

'Nice recovery but a little late. If I had used my blade and not the hilt, you would be dead.' Salaman raised his weapon once more. 'I don't want to see anyone get this close to you Ariela. You have no idea of the enemies you might face in the future.'

'They can't all wield the power of our God though father, just as you can't.' Ariela raised her hands as the tingling sensation began in her fingers. A blaze of light sparked between thumb and forefinger as Salaman raised his palm in the air, words struggling to leave his lips

'We have a quest Salaman. Can you join me in my rooms?' Ariela dropped her hand and the sparks flamed out like flickers of flint stone. Both combatants turned around to see a tall and lean woman with tired eyes and sharp but elegant features standing on the balcony overlooking the training ground.

'Can I come this time? You know I am ready!' Ariela begged her father's retreating back as he took the worn stone stairs to the Old Shiloh Fortress battlements.

'You know that will be up to your mother.' Salaman smiled at Ariela's frustration.

'Yes, but you can convince her. I am eighteen now.' Ariela jumped up and down, clapping her hands together like an excited child.

'Yes, eighteen and way past marrying age.'

The hit was not a surprise but the speed at which it struck caught the fighting veteran unprepared. He groaned as the air surged out of his lungs and frantically tried unsuccessfully to regain his breath.

'I am sorry father, but you absolutely deserved that.' Salaman held up his hand in feigned surrender.

'Will you two stop wasting time! I need to see you Salaman, you too Ariela.'

Ariela could not wipe the grin from her face. 'Finally, mother will give me a quest. I can serve the One True God. You have no idea how the other Priestesses treat me.' Ariela spoke as her father moved ahead of her taking the last of the stairs two at a time.

'I know exactly how they treat you, just like the Princess you are.'

'I'm a Priestess, not a damned Princess. Mother left that all behind, so have I. I want to fight evil, serve God, use the divine powers I was given.' They arrived outside a large oak door as Ariela almost bumped into her father having lost herself in her excitement.

'Your romantic dreams are just that Ariela, dreams. Moloch is a *real* demon. I saw your mother and Aunt nearly die by his hand. Your mother lost someone very close to her that day and has never truly recovered.'

'Yes, but mother and Aunt Francesca won. The Demon died.'

'The Demon didn't die Ariela. He retreated. His servant died and so did many good people that day. Try not to over romanticise what we do. Your mother would do anything to protect you from the darkness she has seen.'

'But that is what the Priestesses train for, to triumph over evil. The girls here have been on many dangerous quests and still I am left on the side-lines, embarrassed and ashamed.'

Salaman stopped to look at his daughter. Her eyes were slightly puffy and red as she held back tears. He reached out and tucked a small fly-away piece of hair back into her loose braid. 'Your mother has used her quest to distract her from her brother, the laws of Israel and her loss Ariela. To lose you would end her so don't be surprised if you never get to go on anything more than a diplomatic errand.'

Salaman patted her shoulder and opened the door to the High Priestess's office before his daughter could protest. 'You called my love.' Salaman bowed extravagantly and smiled.

Ariela followed her father into her mother's study and waited, her impatience evident to everyone except her. Nina smiled at Salaman's antics as she pulled back her loose hair in a leather tie and began to pace the dark wooden floor. Finally, pulling her long pony tail over her shoulder, she sighed and took a seat while indicating with her open hand for Salaman and Ariela to join her.

Both father and daughter took a seat in the two ornate chairs before Nina's desk — relaxing into the embroidered purple fabric covering of the soft cushions. They were faded, but still more beautiful than any other piece of furniture in the room.

Finally, Ariela could hold her excitement no longer. 'What is our quest mother?'

Nina smiled softly at her daughter's enthusiasm. 'It is not so much a quest as a task my darling girl. I have a letter here from Jerusalem.' Nina looked at Salaman's questioning gaze and forced herself to continue. 'The King requests you broker a peace between Israel and the Philistines.'

'No one can ever hope to broker such a peace mother. Both nations have no give and will fight for ever.' Ariela looked to her father for confirmation. 'We have spoken of this often haven't we father?'

'Yes, we have my dear. I spent much of my youth travelling to avoid such futile fighting. But I am not sure we are talking about war here, are we Nina?' Ariela saw the concern in her father's eyes and swung back to look at her mother as she continued to try and explain.

'It is a political proposal so to speak and one I am not sure we can refuse. David is still King and I am his sister.' Nina continued trying to emit a calm she did not feel.

'For goodness sake Nina, we knew this day would come. Stop delaying and tell Ariela what *the King* wants.' Salaman tried to hide his anger, but he spat his words ferociously.

'I know my darling, but how can we avoid it?'

'I am right here you know. What on earth is going on?' Ariela stood now, hands on hips and began to pace the study floor, kicking the faded woven rug with her foot in frustration. 'I am eighteen and still you keep me like a mushroom, in the dark.'

'Your uncle, the King,' Nina halted, trying to compose the words.

'Yes, the kind of King who lets his own sons murder each other and rape their sister.' Salaman was furious but as he saw the hurt in Nina's eyes he softened his features and dropped his eyes in apology.

'David has promised your hand to the Philistine Prince in exchange for trade and a peace treaty.' Nina blurted out the request she had been praying would never come.

'He what!'

'We will find a way around it Ariela, you have my word.' Salaman stood and embraced his daughter who struggled with frustration and fear until the tears started to fall and the safety of her father's embrace seeped into her soul.

Chapter 2

Ariela ran around the old fortress battlement in the relentless heat. Servants and Priestesses avoided her as she rushed past them, her eyes unseeing and her body following a well-worn path automatically.

'Where on earth did you go Narayana? I need your help now. One of your little black holes to the void could open up and swallow me right now and I could escape this nightmare.'

'Ariela! Wait for me.' Salaman jogged up behind his daughter and slowed his pace to match hers. 'I know you're angry. We will figure this out.'

'I wish Narayana were here. He could move me to Egypt or across the sea to somewhere else, anywhere else would do.'

'Yes, the little Holy man could, but when you return the problem will still be here.'

'This is what you expected would happen when you said I would do nothing more dangerous than a diplomatic errand, isn't it?'

Salaman continued to run alongside his daughter without speaking for a time. 'Yes, we knew the day would come. You are still a Princess. The only reason your mother wasn't married off was because she was carrying you. She was too far along. If she hadn't been, David would have found her a husband even though she didn't love anyone else.'

'But she loved you… why didn't you marry her?'

'It's a long story Ariela, and your mother is a complicated woman.'

'I've got time, well until the royal guards come to collect me to take me to my wedding.' Ariela tried to smile but it was forced and Salaman patted her gently on the shoulder as they passed another group of Priestesses who seemed more interested in gossip than training.

'You are the talk of the fortress now you know — a Princess in waiting.'

'I preferred it when everyone simply gossiped about how spoilt I was, but now you are trying to change the subject. Why did you and mother never marry?'

'Nina loved a man once. He died at the battle we spoke of earlier, where your mother and Aunt and Uncle Martinez saved the Prince of the Hittites and restored his throne to him.'

'I had no idea. She never spoke of him.'

'She wouldn't.'

Ariela had a burning question but she couldn't ask it of her father.

'You are my child.' Salaman spoke as though he read her thoughts. 'Your mother and I had a rather tumultuous relationship at first. I loved her from the moment I saw her, but she was heartbroken and although we have had many happy years together, she refused to marry me for her heart would not take another loss. In truth, it probably doesn't matter if we were married or not, if either of us died now, the other would still be dead inside.'

Ariela slowed her pace and smiled genuinely at her father. 'She does love you, with all her heart now. You should ask her to marry you. Maybe you gave up too easily?'

Salaman frowned at the statement. 'I came here to cheer you up but I think you might have something there. You should stop running, you will burn yourself out.'

'I think you might be right,' Ariela stopped running and lent over to regain her breath. I need to spend some time with God. It's been too long.' Salaman patted her on the back once more and moved along the battlements towards Nina's study.

'I wish you were here Narayana, not for the black hole of escape but for your spiritual guidance. The King is busy making treaties with my life on God's behalf but I can't help thinking this can't be the way God thinks, can it?' Ariela realised she was talking to herself out loud and shook herself back to reality. She climbed down the stairs to the training ground and followed the path around the arena until she came upon the gardens of Shiloh.

The trees were heavy with plump olives, the sky was a cloudless blue with a hint of sunset haze appearing in the west. The young Priestess found a soft patch of grass and lowered her tired body to the ground; the feeling of cool leaves against her cheeks was refreshing.

Ariela struggled to focus her spirit on prayer as her mind raced with thoughts. She placed her hand on her chest and willed her breathing to slow down and relax. The sense of commune failed to come before sleep overtook her.

****

Salaman knocked on the study door and entered. 'That could have gone better.' Nina greeted Salaman by crossing the floor and embracing him. Salaman wrapped his arms around her, sensing her need for comfort.

'I'm sorry I didn't speak well of David. Sometimes I wonder where his loyalty truly lies.'

'You should not ever wonder over that. It lies with God. The only issue is if he is interpreting God's wishes accurately. In truth, the Prophets say God wants utter annihilation of the Philistines, yet David claims that peace can be maintained, so in a way, he is going against God, or so the Prophets would have us believe.'

'So he thinks his interpretation is more accurate than Nathaniel's? Oh that is priceless. That Prophet has issues, serious ones. I think his prophecies come from the Queen, not God.'

'Don't say that too loudly, but to be honest, I think David does too, but he has enemies everywhere. Don't get me wrong, I'm not defending his actions in promising Ariela to the Prince, but I understand his motives.'

'Ariela is angry but she was running off her frustration when I left her. I think she will cope. Is there no way to convince David to change his mind?'

'None that I can think of.'

'What about I return to my old occupation. A little assassination maybe?' Salaman smiled wickedly.

'David!'

'No silly, never. The Philistine Prince.' Salaman winked.

'I'm sure the King of the Philistines has another and another. They breed sons like rats you know.'

'You sound jealous, maybe we should have tried for more children?' Salaman gauged his timing. 'Maybe we should have married after all?'

Nina's smile at Salaman's earlier jest was replaced with wide-eyed shock for only a moment before she laughed. 'Married, after all this time?'

'Why not? I should have asked again, I should have asked every day for the past eighteen years, I should never have taken no for an answer. You deserve respect from your family, from...'

Nina lifted her finger to Salaman's lips and stopped his words mid-sentence. 'The only respect I ever asked for was yours and I have it my love but if you wish to make me your wife, then you had best lock that door over there and we can make the arrangements.' Nina indicated the study door with her head and Salaman's gazed followed.

****

Ariela awoke to the star-filled sky. She shook her head to clear the fog and took in her surroundings. 'For goodness sake.' She rose from the grass, the realisation she had not found the peace she longed for in slumber leaving a bad taste in her mouth. Frustration came with wakefulness as the Priestess tried again to find her spiritual serenity.

Moments sitting on the grass passed with no release so Ariela stood to make her way to her chambers. As she crossed the moonlit training arena, she realised her tension was high. Instead of heading to her rooms, she retrieved a sword from the long bank of weapons in the wooden frames that ran along the edge of the training ground and swung it gently to warm up her muscles. She began a few well practised training manoeuvres, slowly bringing her heart rate up.

As she scuffed her bare feet in the dirt of the arena, sliding from one extended stance to the next, the young Priestess began to feel a sense of serenity reach her spirit. Her limbs became weightless and each movement felt as though she were floating on air.

She could see a light before her vision and her senses could feel and hear a humming vibration deep in her body. The light appeared odd, for she could clearly see the courtyard with its now dark stone walls but before them almost translucent was a ray of brilliance that grew brighter than the sun itself.

'God has heard your call Ariela.' The words boomed into the young Priestess's mind like the sound of raging waters and the girl looked around, sword raised to see if anyone else was outside and could see and hear what she could. 'You have the quest you seek but it will come at great personal cost.'

Ariela had never seen such a sight but she began to feel courageous and fearless. She lowered her weapon and dropped it to the ground. 'Anything to avoid a political marriage, anything my God asks of me, I will do it.'

'Then you must come with me now.'

'But what about my family? They will not understand where I am, if I am safe.'

'They will know you are with me.'

'Who are you?' Ariela could not understand why she felt so calm. The stranger before her was tall and broad shouldered. His skin glowed like glistening water at sunset and beyond his form the light was too bright to look directly into. She should have been petrified, yet her heart was beating steadily and her muscles felt relaxed.

'I am the Angel Raziel.' As if to illustrate his authenticity, Raziel extended his silvery white wings that served to momentarily block the shining glow that surrounded him.

Ariela gasped but did not move away, instead she took a few steps forward with uncontrollable interest. She studied the divine being's features, his robes and his sheer size which were now visible in the shadow of his wings. 'I have never heard of you Raziel. My teachings never included Angels, only demons and divine power.'

'Then you still have much to learn it would seem. Are you ready to start?' The Angel lowered his wings protectively wrapping them around himself and the brightness returned.

'Where are you taking me? What must I do? How do I really know you are a messenger of God?'

'Only you can be sure of your choices Ariela. This offer is for now only for if you do not agree, I must seek another who will. The quest is too important.'

Ariela felt queasy, almost faint. 'No one has seen or spoken of Angels since the times of Enoch. Why do you appear before me now?'

'Are you ready Ariela?' Raziel spoke patiently, almost paternally to the young Priestess as he ignored her question with an amused smile she could feel but not see.

Ariela looked around the only home she had ever known. In the moonlight and with the brightness cast from the Angel, she could see every section of stone wall, all the trees that lined the walkway to the dormitory where the other Priestesses lived.

'I have never truly belonged here.' She spoke softly, almost to herself. She looked to her mother's balcony and saw a dim light in her study. 'It's time I found my own path,' she whispered, 'yes Raziel. I believe I am as ready as I could ever be.'

With her answer the Angel nodded and the world around Ariel blurred into brightness too strong to keep her eyes open. A vibration began in her core that radiated to her fingers and toes before covering her whole outer skin like a film of oil.

Ariela's hair felt like there were lightning bolts all around her and she could not be sure, but she could not feel herself breathing.

Time stood still for the Priestess as an inner peace filled her soul to overflowing. She squeezed her eyes tighter and images flashed before her as the sensation of movement ceased. She held her eyes closed as visions that could only be of the Holy realm appeared to her. The power of the place entered her body like bursts of light and she began to shake with the energy.

'I should not look upon this place but I can't stop the images in my mind Raziel. It's amazing.' She whispered. 'The scrolls of Enoch spoke of this place, the realm of God Himself.' The Priestess held her hands before her, her eyes still scrunched tightly closed, feeling for the Angel but he had not answered and she could no longer feel his presence.

The visions and sensation of weightlessness passed too quickly and the young Priestess began to shiver as a feeling of bitter cold seeped into her bones like the frosts of a desert winter.

Ariela felt around her, touching the hard surface beneath her before opening her eyes to nothing familiar. She was covered in grime as though she had rolled in mud. She lifted her arm to her nose and smelt her skin, balking at the aroma. 'For goodness sake, what is this? Mud?' She sniffed again and almost gagged. 'Dung! Raziel is this Dung?' She turned to question Raziel, her eyes scanning the darkness calmly at first then with a sense of urgency, but there was no sign of the Angel.

Chapter 3

'Raziel. This isn't funny.' Ariela paused, awaiting a reply but none came. She pushed herself to her feet and realised she was not sitting on dirt, but rough stone which rubbed against the soles of her feet.

She looked down at her clothing, patting herself in the low light and almost laughed aloud with the shock. Gone was her Priestess tunic and in its place, she wore a long green dress with a full skirt and a low neckline that left nothing to the imagination. For a moment, the Priestess thought her breasts might escape their confines and she carefully tucked herself in.

Fear touched the young woman in that moment. Raziel was gone, she was in a strange land wearing clothing that begged for more attention than she wanted and now the pangs of hunger were attacking her senses too.

'How much lass?' The voice came from behind the Priestess and she jumped at the deep and unwelcomed sound.

'How much for what?' Ariela turned to face the source and was met with dark brown moody eyes and a hawk like nose.

'Don't play dumb missy. It's been a while and I'm in no mood for games.' The man moved in and pushed Ariela hard against the coarse stone wall of the alleyway. He wore a leather kilt and at his side, a short sword rubbed against the Priestesses thigh as the soldier scrambled to lift the girl's skirt.

The Priestess was stunned for only a heartbeat before her father's voice spoke into her mind. *Your enemies will not always be so kind as to afford you the perfect weather.* Or the perfect circumstance it would seem.

Ariela smiled as the soldier became aroused but she did not panic. Instead she lifted the man's weapon clear of the scabbard while she pretended to fumble with his kilt.

'Now that is more like it.' The dark eyes were hooded with a creased brow of confusion as the man's own sword entered his ribs. The air left his lung as blood bubbled up through incoherent words.

'I don't come so cheaply.' Ariela did not stop to draw the sword clear, instead, she scanned the alley for witnesses. She heard voices drifting on the night air. The accents were strange and even the smell of foliage that reached her senses was unfamiliar.

Ariela realised with shock that the soldier had not been speaking Hebrew, but a language she had never heard before, yet she had not struggled to understand him. *'I will do what I can Ariela, but I cannot be seen.'* Raziel's words spoke into her mind, unheard by the world around her. She smiled with relief for only a moment before her anger rose.

'What is it you wish of me?' The young Priestess tried unsuccessfully to keep her words civil.

'You will know when the times comes child, but for now you need to move on. The soldier's friends are looking for him'.

Ariela did not wait, she moved out of the alley into the market place just as a small group of soldiers with white horse-hair plumed helmets brushed past her.

The Priestess's adrenalin was in full flight and she had to force herself to remain calm. She reached out with her talent, seeking calm.

'You are strong for a wee lass.' Ariela swung around to find another stranger staring her down. The old lady had raven black hair and pale skin. The Priestess backed away from the piercing blue eyes that appeared threatening.

'No need to fear me lass. I heard your call.' The old woman continued, smiling through blackened teeth. Ariela tried not to cringe, but the old woman's smile only grew wider.

'I don't know you. I can't possibly have called you.' Ariela was wary, yet she could sense the power emanating all around the strange woman. The question remained — was she a threat or not?

'You will come to know me. For now, how about you come with me for a hot meal and we can talk?' The old woman nodded towards a narrow stone walkway as she spoke.

Ariela didn't speak. She was afraid her voice might betray her. Instead, she nodded and indicated with a wave for the old hag to lead the way.

A roar erupted from the alleyway as the soldiers drew weapons and called for more guards. The marketplace thinned out as evening revellers and stall holders alike began to pack up, spurred on by more soldiers appearing.

'As I said lass, you are strong for a wee one.' The old woman smiled knowingly over her shoulder as she spoke in hushed tones.

Ariela followed the old woman whose well-worn and frayed cape swayed as she walked. She moved briskly despite her gnarled and weathered wooden walking stick.

Ariela sniffed the air and her eyes darted from side to side. She tried to stay calm but the unfamiliar surroundings were intimidating. The Priestess tugged at the top of her dress trying desperately to cover more of herself. She released her braid and pulled her long thick hair over her shoulders and face, trying to become invisible.

A sudden thought had her running to catch up to the old woman. 'You can understand me!'

'Yes.' The old woman looked to her left at the young Priestess, a frown upon her face.

'And I can understand you!' Ariela pushed her inquiry.

'Yes.' This time the stranger's stare was questioning, as though she were speaking with a simpleton.

Ariela realised Raziel had not only helped her understand, but had somehow made her Hebrew into whatever language these local people spoke.

'That's amazing.' The Priestess shook her head with genuine respect for the Angel's powers.

'What is amazing?' The old woman continued to eye Ariela warily.

'I don't know where I am.' Ariela whispered. 'I don't speak your language yet you can understand me.' The Priestess had no idea why she was sharing this revelation with the old woman, but she felt she was safe to do so.

'Ah, now I understand. We will speak of this in my village.' The old woman lifted her makeshift walking cane and pointed ahead of her into the darkness.

Ariela became aware of her surroundings once more. The cobbled streets had given way to dirt paths and dingy older homes made of wood shored up with clay. The homes were more randomly placed around the country side and Ariela realised they had left the township.

They walked on without further discussion as Ariela's stomach did the talking for her. She smiled as the old woman chuckled good naturedly.

Sounds of music and cheers of revelry flowed into the darkness as Ariela saw the glow of a small village fire surrounded by rough wooden shacks come into view.

As the old woman guided the Priestess through the festivities, Ariela caught sight of a small group of young men — mugs of ale in hand — cheering one another on as they threw large rocks into the air.

Ariela kept her head down, but looked sideways from the corner of her eye at the group. With his reddish fair hair and broad shoulders, there was one youth who stood out amongst his fellows.

He gazed at the Priestess, hoisted his ale high in the air and grinned drunkenly in her direction as she passed. Ariela's eyes darted to the ground at her feet with lightning speed and she heard the young man laugh loudly.

As the old woman opened the door to her weathered home, Ariela cast a final quick look over her shoulder at the young men before moving inside the dark and musty doorway.

The old woman flicked her fingers and the fire burst into flames. Ariela jumped back and gasped, while the woman chuckled quietly at the girl's shock.

'Have you not seen this done before lass?' The old woman placed her cane in a rack by the wall and proceeded to walk unaided to the heavily worn wooden table before the hearth.

Ariela was speechless. She had spent her life hiding her gifts from outsiders. 'I am not sure how I should answer that questions. I don't know you.'

'Wise. We live in strange times.' The woman spoke wistfully as though trying to remember a time when she didn't have to be so wary.

'What is your name?' Ariela changed the subject. Discussing her gifts outside of Shiloh had always been considered unwise.

'I am called Morrigan.' The blackened grin reappeared.

'Thank you for your generosity Morrigan. My name is Ariela.'

'I know your name lass.' Morrigan grinned at Ariela's open mouth.

'How could you possibly know my name?'

'I will make you some food and we will talk about what you do and do not know about why you are here. You are the answer to many prayers my dear and when I sensed your presence, I felt truly blessed by the goddess to be chosen to aid you.'

Ariela's stomach grumbled once more and Morrigan smiled.

'Food then sleep; we will talk more in the morning.'

Chapter 4

Ariela could not sleep. She could hear the games the young men were playing outside and there was a piece of her that longed to join them. Yet she was a foreigner to these people and knew nothing of their customs.

The red-headed young man had begun to sing a haunting melody that drifted throughout the small village. He captivated the attention of all his comrades as Ariela watched him from the cottage window. There was a deep red aura that surrounded his entire body and the ground throughout the village pulsed pure energy in response. 'There is the power of God here. I can feel it.' Ariela spoke softly to herself. 'I wish you would tell me what you want Raziel.'

The Priestess knew she needed rest. Her body ached and she could hear her own heart beating in her ears as though her blood was struggling to labour around her body. She sat on the floor of the small room Morrigan had offered her and willed her mind to calmness. She focused on the fire in the hearth; watching the flames twist and twirl like exotic dancers.

But Ariela struggled to relax as images of her uncle and her parents flashed before her eyes. Thinking of her uncle only served to frustrate the Priestess and the visions of her mother and father saddened her. She missed them both and was worried about how they would manage with her gone.

Ariela gave up on any meditation, instead she moved to her cot and rolled the blanket up around her shoulders. She focussed on the words and melody of the song and tried to make sense of them.

As sleep took her, visions replaced her rest. Ariela murmured in her sleep as fear touched her dreams. Soldiers with metal studded breast plates and large rectangular shields marched in formation. The vision blurred to reveal red pools where wings of gold and white floated on the surface, sinking slowly until they were replaced with bubbles of blood.

Raziel appeared, a bright ethereal light radiated from his hands but his image was replaced with Ariela's as the powerful blasts left her hands, hitting the soldiers and exploding on impact.

A man with a face that shone so brightly that Ariela couldn't make out his expression spoke to her, but she could not hear his words. He swept his arm in a gesture which encouraged her to look and as the young Priestess scanned her surroundings all she could see was the village burning and children running and crying.

The red-haired warrior stood by the fire swinging a long silver sword of a size Ariela had never seen As

the sword circled above his head, white light burned
hotter than the biggest forge fire forcing the Priestess to
shield her eyes.

As quickly as the vision had come, all was calm, as
though a raging storm had passed and the earth was
washed clean.

A voice like the Angel hummed in her mind but it
was a woman's words that reached her. *Save the magic
Ariela. The God of Light, the bringer of peace has called you.*

Chapter 5

Rays of warm sunlight filtered through the open window and Ariela groaned as she stretched herself awake.

She did not feel refreshed. Her world still felt as though it were spinning out of control and her dreams had not aided in her composure. She looked around the room that appeared less foreboding in the daylight. There was a planter box of bright flowers below the window and Ariela could smell the fragrance wafting into the room on the light breeze.

'Are you rested well?' Morrigan asked as she knocked on the door frame of Ariela's makeshift room.

'I wouldn't exactly say rested, but I did manage to get some sleep. It's been a whirlwind night.'

The old woman smiled affectionately, showing more of her corroded teeth. 'Come, have something to eat and we can talk.'

'Can you introduce me to the warrior I saw last night?' Ariela had no idea where her boldness had come from except she knew she wasn't used to censoring her behaviour.

'Of course lass. Culaan has that effect on many a young woman.' Morrigan waved her finger in the air in warning. 'You just watch that one though, he is a wee bit of a rogue.'

'No, that's not what I meant.' Ariela covered the cot with the blanket as she responded.

'Of course not lass. Of course not. Keep telling yourself that.'

'No! Really! I had a vision last night and he was in it.' Ariela put her hands on her hips defiantly.

'My point exactly. You have not even met the young man and already you dream of him.' Morrigan chuckled loudly.

'No. Oh never mind.' Ariela decided to explain the vision once her stomach was full. The old woman may have been making fun of her, but either way, she needed to know who the red-haired warrior was and what her vision meant.

Ariela had slept in her dress and it was still muddy and was beginning to smell like a sewer trench. In the daylight, she could see that blood had been smeared on the bodice and even a little had managed to land on her exposed breast.

As if sensing her discomfort, Morrigan spoke. 'You can clean up after we have eaten my dear. I have some more appropriate clothes you can wear and there is a stream not far from here. The water will be cool but at least you can wash away some of that street filth.'

'That would be nice. How is it you found me so quickly?'

'I told you. I felt you arrive, quite suddenly really. I must get you to explain how you did that.' Morrigan questioned the Priestess with a raised eyebrow.

'I didn't do anything and I don't think you would believe me if I told you how I arrived.'

'I think I would. We will have to share the truth with one another eventually if we are going to work together.'

The women made their way into the main living area where a fire was smouldering in the hearth and a tripod with a large metal bowl bubbled away offering an aroma that only fuelled Ariela's hunger.

'That smells delicious. I haven't even done any training but I am famished.'

'Training?' Morrigan stirred the pot over the fire.

'Yes, where I come from I would have usually been awake before the sun rose and have already done a full training session with my father.' Thoughts of Salaman made Ariela feel a deep and sudden melancholy. She missed her mother, but her father meant everything to her. He was the sunshine that greeted her every morning, the one who caught her when she fell and the one to constantly encourage her to get back up again.

'What type of training do you mean? Sorcery?'

Ariela's eyes grew wild and she scanned the room for anyone eavesdropping. 'Sorcery is forbidden where I come from. Is it not the same here?'

'You have avoided my questions, but I will answer yours first.' Morrigan scooped out a ladle of cooked oats and spooned them into a carved wooden bowl. She then placed a strange instrument into the bowl and handed it to the Priestess.

'Sorcery was once a part of our people's daily culture. Wise women like myself were revered and honoured for we had powers that could heal, enchant and protect our people.'

There was a long silence while the old woman reminisced and Ariela felt too uncomfortable to interrupt.

'Since the Romans invaded and our people were forced to broker peace, magic has been less in favour.'

'Who are the Romans?' Ariela inquired innocently.

'How can you not know the Romans lass? They have invaded almost every part of the known world. They enslave the people and then move on like a raging storm.'

'I have never heard of them. Where I come from, it is the Torah laws that forbid magic or sorcery as you call it. My uncle the King once thought it was acceptable, when it served his purpose but lately he has been making it difficult for my mother to maintain the Shiloh Priestess Order.

The officials in Jerusalem constantly push for disbanding the Order and continue to forbid women from worship of our Lord.' Ariela couldn't believe she was revealing so much of the political environment to this woman, but the words had spilled out before she could stop herself.

Now as she looked at the vague expression on Morrigan's face she began to panic and she placed her hand on her mouth in the hopes of stifling further prattling.

'You are from Israel?'

'Yes.'

'Who is the King in Israel? Your uncle? Who is your uncle?' Morrigan spoke quickly and a sense of discomfort continued to grow in Ariela's stomach.

'David, my uncle, King David. Second King of Israel.'

'Impossible!'

'What do you mean?'

'Rome rules in Israel Ariela. There have been no Kings in Israel for over five hundred years.'

'That can't be true!' The Priestess pushed her food away and rose. 'What kind of game is this? You bring me here to tell me lies. Am I a prisoner? Am I to be ransomed to my family?' Ariela scanned the room again. She realised there was so much that was unfamiliar now. She looked at the strange eating instrument in her bowl, the metal used on the cooking pot, even the fabric of her dress and she felt even more uncomfortable.

Morrigan raised her hands, palms up in submission. 'I am no threat to you lass. I swear in the presence of the goddess. You are in Galatia amongst the clans of the Gauls.' The wise woman drew the energy from the air around her as she spoke. This girl might be petite but she was powerful, of this Morrigan was sure.

'No, I left my family just last night. I was in the training ground of the fortress at Shiloh. My uncle promised me in marriage and I prayed for a chance to escape.'

Morrigan lifted her hand and blew on her palm toward the young Priestess. The spell was only meant to calm her and put her to sleep but Ariela's reaction was instinctive.

Her body emanated an intense glow and a burst of power exploded from everywhere around the Priestess, throwing the old woman into the air. She landed heavily against the stone mantel. Morrigan tried to speak as she slipped into unconsciousness.

Ariela scanned the room quickly seeing a neat pile of clothing on the sideboard of the wash basin. Without rational thought, the young Priestess seized the clothes and ran.

Chapter 6

Culaan rolled over onto his back and brushed the dirt from his clothes as he reached for a water jug. His mouth tasted like a week-old loaf of mouldy bread and as much as he disliked water, it was the only solution for how his head felt in that moment.

His hand found something wet and chunky and the young warrior chose not to look, instead he continued his search for water. He managed to pull himself into an upright position, leaning against an aged stump by the dying fire as he gulped down as much water as he could manage without taking a breath.

A loud humming sound distracted him and he rubbed his eyes for clarity as a burst of light erupted inside the Druid's home. He usually took no notice of such strange goings on but when the stray woman ran from the cottage he began to wonder.

Against his better judgement Culaan pushed himself to his feet and stumbled towards Morrigan's home. He fell as soon as his feet touched the ground, landing heavily on his knees. Again, he pushed himself upright and this time successfully made his way to the cottage.

'Morrigan! What was all that commotion about?' Culaan knew better than to enter the house of the woman of magic without an invitation but when no answer came he considered he was out of options.

He pushed the door carefully to a fully open position and peered inside. The room was as it usually was, the walls lined with jars of herbs and strange dried animals Culaan chose not to study too closely.

A groan came from his left and the young man spun around to find Morrigan almost unconscious on the dirt floor with a bleeding welt on her head. He refrained from rushing to the woman. To touch a wise woman was forbidden for a man, something that often puzzled Culaan.

'Morrigan, are you alright? Who was the woman? She just ran out of here like her arse was on fire. What did you do to her?'

'Do to her! You are a witless pup!'

'No need for insults woman.' Culaan kept his distance and watched the old woman warily. There was always a certain amount of mystery about the Druids and the young warrior was happy to remain ignorant to their ways.

'Give me a moment to catch my breath.' Morrigan lent against the stone hearth as she pushed herself to her feet. 'You could offer an old woman a helping hand you know!'

'What, so you can turn me into a toad or curse me for eternity? Not likely!'

'Nonsense. Nothing but an old wives tale told to boys to make sure they keep their hands to themselves.'

'Not what I had heard. Don't you lose your powers or something if a man touches you?'

'No, not unless you plan on bedding me boy and for you I might make the sacrifice.'

'That's disgusting!' Culaan screwed up his nose and held his hands up in a makeshift barrier.

Morrigan laughed and became serious suddenly as she recalled Ariela. 'Find the girl for me. Don't approach her, just find her and come for me.'

'I only came in here to make sure you were not hurt. I am not your personal slave you know.' Culaan put his hands on his hips defiantly.

Morrigan raised an eyebrow frowning at Culaan for added dramatic effect. 'Your insolence will not be forgotten lad. Now go and find the girl. She is very important.'

Culaan shrugged, realising the fight was already lost. 'She is rather pretty. Come to think of it, I might enjoy finding her.'

'Keep your hands to yourself Culaan. She is frightened and there is no telling what she will do to you if you catch her by surprise.'

Culaan smiled mischievously. 'A man can live in hope. Any idea where to start looking?'

Morrigan closed her eyes and focussed her energy. 'Give me a moment to seek out her spirit. She may have shielded herself by now, but it is worth a try.'

Chapter 7

Ariela stopped to catch her breath. 'Raziel, where are you?' There was no answer and the young Priestess sank to the ground in the shade of a monstrous tree the likes of which she had never before seen. As she surveyed her surroundings Ariela struggled to fight the sense of loss. Everything was unfamiliar, from the deep and dark greenery, to the strange leaves on the trees, to the temperate weather and the ice-capped mountains in the distance.

The young woman brushed her fingers through the tall grass, plucking the seeds clear in frustration. 'She must be wrong. If the old woman is right, then my family is gone. I need you Raziel. Where are you? You said you would aid me when I needed you! I need you now.' The Priestess wiped a solitary tear from her face and scowled.

Ariela's father's voice spoke into her dark mood, willing her to get back up and fight on. Thoughts of Salaman made her smile as she recalled the many stories he told of his exploits as a young soldier.

She knew there was always more to his past than he had shared, but what he had told her sounded free and frightening all at the same time.

The young Priestess regained her composure and looked at her blood covered clothing and the fresh linen dress and heavy hooded robe the old wise woman had prepared. She recalled their conversation about a stream and decided that if nothing else, she needed to wash away the grime of the night before.

Years of training came to bear as Ariela closed her eyes to focus her talent on her surroundings. Seeking out water had been a rudimentary skill taught to every young novice who entered the Shiloh Order. Finding water could be lifesaving and every young Priestess in training should have enough basic control of their gift to find such a life-giving element.

The young Priestess began to imagine water in her mind. At first she felt nothing until the image of cascading water came to her. The rocks behind the water disappeared into the sky and the water misted into the air as it fell. The scene was glorious, nothing like the palm-rimmed oasis of the desert where Ariela had grown up. Excitement replaced her apprehension. She prayed the water she would find should look as magnificent as her vision.

****

'I cannot find her Culaan. I need you to seek her out. Do not approach her. Just report back to me. She is dangerous.'

'So you said. Why bring her to the village if she is such a threat?'

'Because she is a gift from the Goddess and with her help, the Druid magic will survive the occupation of the Roman Empire.'

'Have you spoken with Owyn about this threat?' Culaan did not get involved with politics or the peace treaty his ancestors made with the Romans but he knew Owyn should know if the Old Druid woman had seen something. 'You're obliged to share your visions and knowledge with Owyn.'

'Don't tell me what I am obliged to do lad. Besides, you are one to talk, you can call him father you know!'

'He is my father by blood only and you should mind your own business.' Culaan tried to stay calm but talk of the clan leader as his father always left a foul taste in his mouth.

Morrigan smiled. The boy knew how to hold a grudge. 'You should mind yours as well.' The Druid conceded 'I have not discussed this with *your father*. I had barely met the girl and certainly have not had the time to assess her skills or her use to the clan.'

'I will find her, then you will tell Owyn what is going on or I will.'

'Just try not to startle her Culaan. The Tectosagii clan needs her, of that I am sure.'

'I will take Genevieve with me. She can help track the girl, you know how much I excel at tracking.' Culaan suddenly smiled mischievously as he ducked through the doorway before the old wise woman could throw anything at him.

The young warrior found Genevieve buried below an armful of shrew as she stripped the skin. She smiled as he approached and casually waved a blood smeared hand in greeting.

'Morning Culaan. How is your head?'

'When I woke up it was shocking and now it's even worse. I need your help Genie' Culaan slumped down on the wooden stool next to a small pile of animals, half skinned, half still covered in fur with dead eyes peering into nothingness. He gazed into the lifeless eyes for a moment, before shifting his attention back to the huntress.

Genevieve stopped what she was doing as she studied her friend's face. Culaan wore a rough beard that looked unkempt and as rogue as the warrior himself. His piercing blue eyes always left all the young women with butterflies skipping around their bellies, but he knew this and used their appeal to his advantage.

'Your head can't possibly hurt that badly Culaan. It's not like you to be so pouty. Can I help?'

'Of course you can. Why else would I be here?'

'My heart bleeds. There I was thinking you had come to visit me and help me clean this lump of meat, but no, you're not even after my body.' Genevieve laughed at the feigned shock on her friend's face.

'I need your renowned tracking skills my dear and you know how much I love to have a pretty woman at my side while I work.'

'More like under your body, but I will play along. What do you want me to track?'

'Not what, more a who.' Genie raised an eyebrow. 'Another pretty woman of course.' Culaan grinned as Genevieve threw a bloodied piece of shrew gizzard right at his head. 'Luckily you are a better tracker than marksman. Meet me at the Birch as soon as you are cleaned up. I need to gather a few supplies and you will attract predators smelling like that.' Culaan winked at Genie as another piece of raw animal left her hand.

Genevieve watched the tall warrior stroll away, his woollen kilt swaying as he moved. She sighed and began hanging the already dressed meat along a drying line in the storeroom. She took one last look as Culaan disappeared from her sight. She sneered good naturedly at her friend's arrogance. There was no denying the fact that he was strong, a very skilled warrior and she would bed him if only he would ask.

Chapter 8

Ariela gazed longingly at the water rushing down the mountainside as she removed her vile and uncomfortable dress. The pool below the cascading water was deep and dark and the Priestess waded in apprehensively. She had no idea how to swim, so she clung to the rocks tenaciously, trying desperately to keep her balance on the slippery bottom as the waters moved around her.

Ariela gasped as the frigid water touched her breasts and goose pimples dotted her torso. She submerged her head quickly and suddenly rushed to scrub away the dirt and blood of the night before.

As she washed her skin, she began to rub more frantically — the face of the dead soldier appearing before her mind's eye. The blood was difficult to remove and the harder it was to wash away, the more desperate Ariela became to be free of the memory.

'You trained me too well father but I wasn't prepared for this.' The soldier's lifeless eyes haunted her memory and she shook her head vigorously, trying to free her memories.

Ariela drowned her thoughts as she plunged her head below the water once more. She held her breath and scrubbed her hair below the surface willing the grime to come free.

She stifled a giggle at the strange sensation of being fully submerged. She surfaced and floated on her back, the feeling of weightlessness a reminder of travelling in her astral form.

'Now that is a sight to behold.'

Ariela sank below the surface and came up choking with her arms folded over her breasts defensively. 'Who the hell are you?'

'I don't believe you are in any position to be asking the questions. Why don't you bring your sexy little body out here so I can get a closer look?' The man smirked in a way that left no doubt as to what a 'closer look' entailed. Ariela supressed a shiver.

'Why don't you come in and get me you ogling piece of camel dung?'

'Camel dung? Now that's novel. We don't get many camels in the mountains lass. You're not from around here, are you!' The stranger circled closer to Ariela but remained on the rock pool edge.

'I'm not coming out, so if you want me, you will have to come in and get me.' Ariela couldn't swim out into the middle because she wasn't sure she would stay afloat. She carefully scanned her surroundings as the stranger grew agitated.

'Well, I usually like my prey kicking and screaming, but maybe I can make an exception for you.' He pulled his dagger out and flipped it threateningly, sneering at the Priestess with every fall of the blade.

Ariela waited patiently. She wasn't coming out of the water unarmed and if that meant sustaining an injury, then so be it. Her father was so right. Enemies really didn't have a good sense of timing. If she ever saw him again, she was going to have to thank him for his sage advice.

Ariela moved to the furthest side of the rock pool, grabbing stones for balance as she half walked, half swam. She found a ledge and stood, her chest barely covered by water. She searched for an escape route, but found nothing.

The knife flew with great speed unexpectedly toward her chest, but her assailant wasn't fast enough. Ariela had been drawing energy from the water and as the dagger flew, she reached out with her spirit, halting it mid-flight. She smiled as she reached up and plucked the weapon from its suspended state.

Her adversary remained momentarily stunned, before slowly drawing his sword. 'I don't know how you did that, but it's time to die pretty one. I had hoped to play with you first,' the man shrugged, 'but I think maybe killing you is a safer and wiser idea.'

****

'Did you hear that?' Genevieve looked over her shoulder as she crept through the undergrowth, Culaan following close behind.

'Yes, voices.' The warrior whispered before nodding for her to move on.

The waterfall was a few paces ahead and as the pair of trackers reached the clearing they stopped.

'We should do something.' Genie said as she took the last step onto the mossy ground that littered the edges of the large pond.

'Load your bow, but don't fire. This could prove enlightening.' Culaan put his hands on his hips without moving towards his sword or the naked woman in the water.

'Stop gawking. We should really help her you know.' Genevieve pulled an arrow from her quiver.

'True, but I can't exactly kill my half-brother. Owyn would be fairly upset. If it gets out of hand, you can shoot that arrow at his feet. Besides, Morrigan said she was dangerous, let's see just how dangerous.'

'Your call. If anyone dies though, I'm telling Owyn it's your fault.'

'What's new!' Culaan smiled but did not take his eyes from the young naked girl as she climbed from the water and began circling toward Reaghan from the far side of the pond.

She held his dagger in her hand and Culaan rubbed his chin thoughtfully as he considered how she had gotten it from him while still in the water.

She moved in on his half-brother like a lion, fast and furiously as Reaghan raised his long sword. Culaan suddenly realised he had waited too long and began to panic. 'Let it fly Genie.'

The arrow flew, landing with a thud at Reaghan's feet. Ariela dived aside, rolling clear of both the arrow and Reaghan's sword.

'Alright, that's enough you two. Reaghan, what the hell are you doing?' Culaan moved towards his half-brother.

'You piss off Culaan! This is between me and the girl.'

'What, let me guess, she refused your charming advances? At what point was that, before or after you threatened her?' Culaan was letting his rage free and that was dangerous for them both.

Genevieve moved toward the girl, another arrow notched and ready. 'Stay calm Culaan, Owyn won't want him dead.'

Reaghan laughed loudly. 'I'm not that easy to kill.'

'Keep lying to yourself Reaghan. We both know Culaan could kill you with one hand tied behind his back.'

Genevieve smiled as she goaded Reaghan and moved between him and the girl, her arrow still notched, her back to the stranger. She felt the tension from the girl, but there was little choice.

'Put the sword down Reaghan.' Culaan forced himself to remain calm.

'Or what!' Reaghan spun the weapon menacingly.

'Don't be stupid Reaghan, you attacked an unarmed naked girl and you expect your father to rule in your favour?' Genevieve yelled, trying to bring sanity to the situation.

Reaghan glared at the huntress. 'She is armed!'

'With your dagger, strange don't you think?'
Culaan spat the accusation.

Reaghan's eyes darted from Culaan to Genevieve and the stranger. He had the look of a cornered rabbit. He had not dropped his sword and Culaan warily moved closer, watching Genevieve and Reaghan closely.

'Reaghan, drop the sword and we walk away with the girl. No one speaks of this again. You have my word.'

Ariela sat on her haunches, her eyes focused on her prey and the dagger at the ready. She took a deep breath to maintain her composure and crouched low to cover her nakedness, waiting apprehensively.

Chapter 9

Reaghan dropped his sword with a heavy thud and Genevieve released her bolt and turned to the naked woman as she replaced the unused arrow to her quiver.

'Are you alright?' Genevieve placed her bow back over her shoulder and bent down to speak. 'He's a pig, but a formidable fighter. You did well.'

'Can I have my clothes?' The girl pointed to a neatly folded dress and robe sitting on a rock by the water's edge.

'Of course, sorry.' Genevieve moved toward the clothing, past Reaghan apprehensively giving him a wide berth and watching every move he made.

'Back away Reaghan and we will be on our way in a moment. You can collect your sword once we are gone.' Culaan levelled his short-sword at his brother's chest and waved it toward the far side of the clearing.

Reaghan appeared to have gained some composure. He moved away warily as ordered, sneering at his brother with obvious disdain. 'You're still the bastard son and always will be.'

Culaan grinned. 'And what makes you think that bothers me Reaghan? I don't think you get your manners from our father.'

'Enough, both of you.' Genevieve grumbled as she moved back past them toward Ariela with the clothing. She handed the bundle to the girl and turned her back while the Priestess threw the dress over her head and wrapped the robe around her shoulders.

She smiled as she watched Culaan suddenly distracted watching the girl out of the corner of his eye. The young huntress had to admit, she was beautiful. Her body was lean and taut revealing the source of her speed and skill.

'My name is Ariela.'

Genevieve turned around at the sound of the girl's voice. 'Nice to meet you Ariela. My name is Genevieve and this is Culaan.' The tracker waved her hand toward her friend who nodded, his sword still held out at the ready, his bare bicep rippling with the strength required to hold his weapon extended for such a long time.

'Let's get out of here.' Culaan indicated the brush behind them with a nod of his head and Genevieve moved off with Ariela close behind.

Culaan gave his brother one last warning look before disappearing into the treeline behind the girls.

The group travelled in silence, each with their own thoughts. Ariela waited until they were well away from the waterfall before speaking. The sound of the crashing water became a distant memory that somehow saddened the Priestess.

'Where are we going?'

'Back to the village.' Culaan's short answer made Ariela look behind her. His expression was difficult to read.

'I didn't need you to save me you know!'

'That could be true, but if you had killed Reaghan, your life with our Clan would have come to an abrupt end.'

Ariela frowned to herself. Why on earth was he protecting a man who would molest a woman with no provocation. 'Clan?' The Priestess spoke aloud.

'Yes, don't you have a Clan?' Culaan frowned with confusion.

'I don't know what a Clan is. Everything I know is gone. I have no idea where I am, how I got here or where my family is.'

Culaan raised his eyebrows as the girl spoke over her shoulder to him. 'How can you not know where you are?'

'I'm from Israel. Where is that in relation to this place?' Ariela moved over a rocky outcrop. Navigating the rough ground made it impossible to speak face to face.

'Israel! I have heard of it. The Romans have taken it over just like everything else but I have never been there.'

'So, you're a Judean?' Genevieve turned to look excitedly at Ariela as she joined the conversation.

'A what!' Ariela's response exploded with more aggression than she intended.

'A Judean, descendent of the Israelites who were exiled from Judah and then returned to Jerusalem before

it was later overthrown by the Roman Empire.'
Genevieve frowned at Ariela's confusion.

'I have no idea how you know all that, but no, I'm an Israelite, niece to King David, daughter of Nina, High Priestess of the Order of Shiloh.'

Genevieve and Culaan exchanged confused expressions before bursting out in laughter. 'You're either delusional or you have travelled a long way. You could call me something of a history scholar but the place and people you speak of haven't been around for over seven hundred years.' Genevieve stopped and faced Ariela, hands on her hips and a questioning gaze.

'Well I'm not insane and I assure you, I know who my family is. So, somehow I have been moved through time and I have a pretty good idea who is responsible. When I get my hands on Raziel, he had better hope his divine power is at its best.'

Culaan and Genevieve looked at each other once more as the girl ranted. 'I think we had better get you back to Morrigan, she will make sure you get the help you need.' Culaan pointed for Genevieve to continue, quickly!

****

'How did Marcellus die in the middle of peace times?' The Senator was outraged. 'How am I going to explain this to my sister? The Ankyra region had been relatively peaceful. It must be that crucifixion at Golgotha that has everyone on edge.'

'Nothing to do with killing the Judean your Grace. Marcel was drunk and whoring. Someone saw a young woman leave the alley just before we arrived. Looks like he tried to get a taste of a rather vicious wench.' The soldier had his helmet under his arm and smiled wicely at his own revelation.

'Be careful Dominic. You know Marcellus was my nephew.' The Senator rose from his large oak desk and walked over the plush furs to the side table and poured himself a goblet of wine. He took a long gulp and placed the drink down as his mind mulled over ideas.

'We will have to come up with a more valorous story for his mother, but in the meantime, track down the whore and bring her to me.'

'As you wish.' Dominic saluted the Senator and turned on his heels to leave, but stopped as a sudden thought came to him. 'What if she doesn't come quietly your Grace, can we…' the soldier turned back to his leader and shrugged, 'you know, use whatever means necessary?'

'Do what you have to do but bring her alive. I want to know how a whore kills a soldier of the Empire and calmly walks away without a second thought.'

'Yes Sir.' Dominic smiled wickedly.

Chapter 10

Morrigan was waiting in the village when Culaan returned. She had sensed Ariela was safe, but there was so much riding on the young woman that she couldn't help but be fearful something untoward might happen to her.

'What on earth took you so long?'

'Lovely to see you too Druid. It took Genevieve a little while to track her and then Reaghan had beaten us to the girl.'

'My name is Ariela. I have already told you that. Are you always so rude?'

Morrigan looked from the Priestess to the Warrior, a smile appearing on her lips. 'I see you two have gotten to know one another better. Culaan, did you leave your charm at home this morning?'

Genevieve chuckled from behind her friend, who spun around and scowled at her. 'What?' Genie held her hands up in defence. 'You can be a little abrasive at times. I don't think the hang-over is doing him any favours either.' Genie grinned as she looked past Culaan to the Druid.

'Enough, all of you. Is Reaghan alright?' Morrigan interrupted without returning the Huntress's smile.

'Why is everyone so worried about that rat? Really, he tried to rape me and you all seem to be defending him. What kind of place is this? My Uncle would have cut off his hand or his manhood for such behaviour.' Ariela gritted her teeth without bothering to cover her disgust.

'None of us condone his behaviour, but we explained the politics to you. A blind person should be able to see when it's wise to keep their mouth shut.' Culaan turned to leave. 'She is all yours Morrigan, complete with her delusions of time travel and obvious simplistic understanding of what it takes to keep the peace. Maybe you really are a King's niece, you certainly act like a spoilt royal brat.'

Genevieve looked at Culaan's back with confusion. She moved to Ariela and placed a hand on her arm gently. 'It's all very complicated between Culaan and his family. None of that was really directed at you. It was nice meeting you Ariela.' The young Huntress moved away to follow Culaan, collecting a jug of ale from Morrigan's table and hoisting it above her head, while looking at the Druid for permission to take it with her.

Morrigan nodded her approval and understanding as Genevieve left.

Ariela opened her mouth to speak but nothing sensible came to mind. She returned her attention to Morrigan, still unsure of the woman's intentions.

'I am sorry about earlier lass. I was only intending to release a calming spell. I should have known better than to use magic on you.' The Wise woman moved forward and extended her hand to Ariela. 'Can we start again?'

Ariela looked at the hand unsure of what to do. Morrigan saw her confusion and smiled. 'It is a greeting amongst our people. Place your hand in mine and we exchange introductions or pleasantries.' Morrigan took the young Priestess's hand in hers. 'Like this' She shook Ariela's hand gently. 'Lovely to see you safe Ariela.'

Ariela could feel the woman's energy and a bright green aura filled her with a sense of trust. 'Thank you for trying to keep me safe Morrigan.'

'Of course. You have a great purpose to fulfil and keeping you safe is very important to me and my people. Now what is all this about royal brats?' Morrigan grinned.

'When I left you yesterday, I was beginning to understand my world had shifted, but after talking with Genevieve and Culaan, I think Raziel might have dropped me not only a long way from home, but in a different time. I don't understand why he would do that!'

'The Angels and the Gods communicate with each other I'm sure. I suggest Raziel knew we needed your help.'

'You speak of matters that would be blasphemous where I come from.'

'You mean *when* you come from.' Morrigan smiled. 'A lot has changed since King David ruled in Israel. The Israelites have been assimilated into the Roman Empire and they have huge temples of worship in all the major cities of the Empire. They pay their taxes and the Romans, up until recently have given them a relatively free reign with their religion. The line between the Roman Gods and the Israelite Gods is getting blurrier every day. You see, your people have grown to value money as much as the Romans do.'

'You said up until recently.' Ariela wanted to understand this new world she was living in.

'Yes, the Roman's crucified a man who claimed to be the Messiah of your god Yahweh. Now that on its own would not have been a huge issue, but it has set the Romans in opposition to both the Pharisees and Sadducees and there is a new branch of your religion further at odds with all of them. There has been a great deal of political and religious upheaval leading up to and since the Prophet's death.'

'You speak of things that don't exist where I come from. There is the Torah law and the King. The King has ultimate religious say, but he has a counsel made up of many religious leaders, members of the military and even my Aunt, a Priestess. He consults with them often for their guidance.'

'I understand it is a lot to take in Ariela, but the Romans are more powerful than your Uncle the King could ever have dreamt to be and we live in a time when religion and politics are one in the same. With the influence of the Pharisees and Sadducees on the Roman Emperor, the Druids have been targeted.'

'You will first have to explain to me what on earth a Druid is. I heard Culaan call you that, and you spoke of magic… what does it all mean?'

'Come, let us go inside. You must be hungry. I think we probably need to talk more about how you got here, before we get too wrapped up in the political environment of Ankyra.'

Reaghan ran his finger down the edge of his dagger as he watched the foreign woman go inside the old wise woman's cottage.

'You are as good as dead pretty one.' He licked his lips as he whispered into the brambles around him.

Ariela felt a chill run down her spine and the hair on the back of her neck sprung to attention. She stopped walking for a moment and scanned the village perimeter.

'What is it?' Morrigan asked

'Nothing, I'm sure it's nothing.' Both women entered and Morrigan closed the cottage door.

Chapter 11

'She's very pretty.' Genevieve smiled as she took another long swig of her ale. 'I can understand why you turn into a blundering fool around her.'

Culaan didn't answer, he gulped down the jug of ale and slammed it down on the table. 'Another one and bring me some roast meat. I'm ravenous.' He called out loudly, his words slurring slightly from too much ale, consumed too fast.

Culaan was distracted as the tavern door opened and Reaghan entered. Genevieve caught sight of him and slapped Culaan on the back to keep his attention on food and ale. 'I am feeling a little hungry too come to think of it. It's been a big day.' A barmaid with tired eyes and wide hips swayed up to their table.

'You have a large account here Culaan. You sure you got the means to pay for more ale and food?' She placed another big jug of ale down as she spoke.

'I always pay my debts Rowena. You can tell that man of yours I can always cut a winter's supply of firewood for his ovens or catch him some game for his roaster.'

'There is truth in that Culaan. I'll fetch you some meat.'

Culaan slapped her on the backside as she made to walk away and smiled when she scornfully objected to his behaviour. 'You protest too much Row. You know you love it!'

'You're a rogue Culaan, you know that don't you!' The barmaid waved her finger and smiled to soften her words.

'But a more handsome rogue you will never find.' Culaan saluted the woman with his fresh mug of ale and gulped it down greedily.

'You really should take it easy. Kelven might take offence at you handling his woman that way.' Genevieve looked seriously at her friend. He could be so self-destructive at times but she cared about him more than she liked to admit.

Reaghan sauntered over toward Culaan. Genevieve saw him approaching and shook her head to discourage him, but he was in no mood to heed her advice. She could feel him gloating and it appeared to her as though everyone in the tavern held their breath when he spoke to his half-brother.

'That was rude of you today Culaan. The girl is a foreigner and when father finds out you have kept her from the clan counsel, you might wish I had killed her.'

'Killing isn't really your specialty though is it brother? Besides, I think she is out of your league in more ways than one.' Culaan smiled without looking at his brother. Genevieve was surprised he remained calm, but Reaghan was bubbling with contempt.

'Reaghan! Starting a fight in the tavern won't do either of you any good. You know Owyn will have to punish you both if you do any damage.' Genevieve pushed Reaghan gently on the chest, physically trying to create some distance between the brothers.

'She's right you know.' Culaan spoke into his ale, his back still contemptuously facing his brother. 'Owyn might not like me but he *loathes* you. Heir or not, you are still a twisted bastard.'

Reaghan growled as he launched his attack, pushing Genevieve aside. Even intoxicated, Culaan was an instinctive fighter. The warrior moved effortlessly to the side, opening a space that Reaghan fell right through. Unbalanced and surprised, the fight was over in a heartbeat. Culaan had Reaghan's head pinned to the rough wooden bench and he was pressing down firmly.

Reaghan flailed his fists trying desperately to reach a weapon. Culaan moved to the right of his brother and grabbed his fist, shoving it hard against his back. He moved in behind Reaghan's back and lent in, jabbing the man's right arm up as hard as he could, while still holding his head firmly against the bench.

'Don't ever come at me again *brother* or I will kill you. You understand?' He whispered into his ear almost lovingly. 'I should do to you what you wanted to do to that poor girl today but you might enjoy it too much.' Culaan lifted his brother's head by the hair and smacked it back down firmly. Reaghan's legs gave way and the man crumpled to the ground.

'Sorry about that Row. Add it to my account.' Culaan called out across the tavern as he kicked his brother in the stomach. He turned to Genie, 'I have lost my appetite. Let's get out of here.'

Genevieve scanned the faces in the tavern and they were nothing short of stunned. The Huntress smiled as she knelt next to Reaghan. He was barely conscious. 'I did warn you to leave.' She patted him on the shoulder and followed Culaan, nodding to patrons as they made a wide path for their Chieftain's half son and his best friend.

****

Owyn sat upon a fur covered high backed chair large enough for a man twice his size. To his side stood two of his trusted counsellors and on the far wall of the Chieftains chambers, a large table took pride of place. Above the table weapons were mounted including the legendary leader Ortagion's infamous double-edged axe.

Owyn allowed the silence to linger as Reaghan stood before him. 'What were you thinking, goading your brother? Are you insane?' The Chieftain resisted the urge to rise to his feet.

'Half-brother.' Reaghan corrected as he looked up through one half-open eye, the other bruised, black and swollen shut. He flexed his shoulder as he waited for his father to calm down.

'Yes, my half. You pompous pain in the arse.'

Reaghan wanted to say what he was thinking but he held his tongue. Instead he decided to distract his father. 'They are harbouring a stranger. I was just going to suggest he tell you about her, that's all.'

'A her? That explains a lot. You and women shouldn't be in the same space lad.' Owyn looked mournfully at Reaghan as he spoke. 'You know you have absolutely no self-control. What did you do? Try to rape his woman again?'

'No, I came upon her, the stranger and when I made to arrest her, she fought me. Culaan interceded and took her to the village. I followed and found that she is residing with the Druid. I know how much you dislike their type, so I thought you should know.'

Owyn shook his head. It all sounded too rehearsed for him and as much as it pained him to admit it, he knew there was more to the story than Reaghan would ever share. 'Don't bring my quarrel with the Druids into this. I will send word this afternoon and make the arrangements to meet this stranger. If Morrigan is involved, it is bound to mean trouble for the Tectosagii Clan.'

'When are you going to give that woman up to the Romans? They are hunting out all her kind. Why do you protect her?' Reaghan frowned his confusion.

'She is still of our clan lad and we need to protect our own. The Romans bring money and trade but they don't understand our gods or our culture. They rape every civilisation they come across and there are no true gods left to oppose any of them. I play along to appease them and keep my clan safe lad and for no other reason. They will not wipe out the Druids while I live.'

'Since when have the gods opposed any of our enemies? They are nothing more than myths — stories told to scare children.'

'You still have so much to learn. My only hope is you never find the need to learn it.'

Reaghan frowned at his father's words 'Do you want me to send word to the village to bring the lass to you?'

'Of course I don't. You have done enough. Go find a whore and Reaghan, this time, leave her in one piece. You understand me?' Owyn pointed at his son's chest and Reaghan nodded his understanding before turning to leave.

The words tumbled around his head but they never left his lips. His hand brushed past his sword hilt but he forced himself to walk on. He hadn't even left the room before conversations continued between his father and his advisors.

Chapter 12

'Dorran, find a lad to get a message to Morrigan. We need to see this lass and find out what the old hag is up to.' A broad-shouldered man with kind eyes stepped forward, taking the two steps to the Chieftain's platform with agility that belied his age.

'Of course Owyn.' The man showed no reverence or use of the Chieftain's title but the casual manner bothered neither man. 'What about Reaghan?' Dorran rubbed his chin as he spoke, choosing his words carefully.

'What do you suggest my friend? He is my flesh and blood.' Owyn's face was sullen and his eyes tired. He reached for a goblet of wine and took a long gulp before placing it back on the side table, fingering the stem of the metal cup and not yet willing to let it go.

'True, but when a herd has a diseased animal, it either kills it, or leaves it behind to die.' Dorran's tone was conversational and his smile warm.

'We are a clan not a herd and no one is leaving Reaghan behind to die.' Owyn sighed and leaned into his high-backed chair, taking a slower more relaxed sip of his wine as he composed himself.

'I thought beating it out of him when he was young would get the task done, but his mother coddled him. She told him he could have anything he wanted, that he was smarter and stronger than anyone, especially Culaan, and the world was his for the taking.'

'Seems he may have taken her too literally.' Dorran smiled. 'It's a shame that all he wants is women. If he had as much desire for wealth or power, he might be useful.' The man patted his friend on the shoulder as he spoke, his eyes full of genuine sympathy.

'I pray to the goddess for him Dorran, but I think all the old gods are now dead. The Roman's want to rid our people of our faith by killing out the magic. They hate anything that might be more powerful than they are and have no doubt Dorran, the Druids are powerful, or they were when there were enough of them.'

'There are not enough left to rid us of the Romans now. Is it wise to continue to hide the remainder of them? Your family history with them isn't exactly ideal after all. You owe them nothing.'

'You heard me Dorran. No Druid will die at my hand and I will do all in my power to preserve those we have left. It's the principle. Yes, they gave poor counsel to my great uncle Ortagion of the Tolistobgii clan when he tried to unite all the clans, but that is history. We must move forward.'

'But if they hadn't allowed Ortagion's wife Chiomara to be taken and raped, we might all be one clan now.'

'That's not quite how it all unfolded my friend There was betrayal on many sides. There were those amongst the clans who would have given anything to stop a united front against the Roman's. Ortagion preached allegiance to Rome. My great grandfather had other ideas.'

'Are you saying your family orchestrated Chiomara's abduction?'

'I am saying I wasn't there but there have been rumours. The Druids were merely puppets in a plot — each doing what they believed was right for the tribal leader they served.' Dorran inhaled quickly and stepped back from his friend. He opened his mouth to speak but Owyn waved his hand.

'We can't blame the Druids Dorran, they have suffered enough for their naivety. They aided the Romans in putting us under their yoke, but now the Romans have joined the Judeans to wipe out anything that gives hope to the common people and make no mistake Dorran magic brings hope as it has to the new religion where miracles and magic are being spoken of in homes late at night; where love and mercy are preached by the Judean prophet.'

'Then we must play our part to save the Druids and their magic. I'm sorry I doubted your wisdom Owyn.' Dorran bowed. 'I will fetch the lass myself my Lord. I will return with her this evening. Morrigan and I have our own history. She will see me.'

Owyn raised a questioning eyebrow which Dorran answered with a wicked smile. The Chieftain decided not to pursue the issue, he had other matters to worry about

'Thank you my friend. Can you set someone to keeping an eye on Reaghan as a favour to me? Another dead whore is the last thing we need right now, not with Dominic and that bastard Senator breathing down our necks.'

'I will see to it.' Dorran bowed to his Chieftain and left the meeting hall.

****

The room was expansive but dimly lit with tall candelabras that circled the establishment and more candles hanging from ornately carved wooden wheels attached to the roof by chains.

Reaghan looked at the chains and felt a sense of unease wash over him. He shuddered, but made his way past tables and lounges to the long bar that lined the far wall. He licked his lips in anticipation of a shot of something far stronger than ale.

'Reaghan.' The clansman jumped at the sound of his name. He had come here to remain anonymous, unseen by his kin. He turned to see the Roman Centurion Dominic smiling amicably. Out of uniform he was always harder to recognise.

'Can I find you one of our finest ladies for the evening? I could make a recommendation if you like?' Dominic patted the Chieftain's son on the back and smiled as he welcomed him to the long bar. 'How about I get you a drink while you wait?' The man clicked his fingers and the broad and burley barman began to pour ale. Reaghan couldn't be sure, but he thought the barman nodded rather strangely to the centurion.

'Father hasn't been too generous with the coin of late Dominic, I think your tastes might be a little out of my price range. I had planned for a quick shot of something stronger than ale and then I will be on my way.' Reaghan tried not to pout but he knew he had been unsuccessful.

'Nonsense! Consider it a favour amongst friends. I'm sure you can owe me one. I know you are good for it, aren't you?' Reaghan smiled and nodded taking the pot of ale offered him.

'Absolutely! You know I am.'

'In that case, let's top this evening off with a meal and a few more drinks while we are at it hey!' The soldier waved to a young serving girl with a slim waist, voluptuous breasts and long red hair tied back in a thick plait. She listened as he whispered in her ear, then giggled and curtsied before heading back to get the order.

'What did you order?' Reaghan felt uncomfortable as the hairs on his arm rose in protest. He looked back to the barman and observed him avert his eyes quickly.

'I ordered you the Roman treatment. You're in my house now Gaul, you need to learn to enjoy entertainment as the Romans do. A hot bath, a relaxing massage, some food, some wine and whatever else might take your fancy.'

There was no time to ask further questions as the serving woman returned, not with ale or food, but with three scantily clad women. The first had hair the colour of night and bronzed skin that glistened with oil. She wore dark eye liner and her eyes were almost purple.

Her belly button was exposed with sheer fabric falling from her hips to the floor like ribbons.

The other two were both Galatian of Gaul decent. Their hair was red with golden highlights, blue eyes and pale porcelain looking skin. Reaghan's breath caught in his throat as the three young women moved to encircle him, their hands touching his body and sending electrifying shock waves to the pit of his stomach and beyond.

'I think you have him speechless ladies. Take him to the bathhouse and remember, Reaghan is a friend of mine, so give him the Roman treatment. Only the best for my friends.'

The dark-haired woman collected Reaghan's hand in hers and led him as the two Galatian women wrapped their arms around his waist, one on either side. The young heir of Ankyra allowed his imagination to begin working on what one man was supposed to do with three women at once. He smiled as he boldly took the woman on his right into his one free arm and nuzzled her neck. She giggled good naturedly in response.

As Reaghan moved away, four Roman soldiers joined Dominic. They wore full uniform and carried their swords indiscreetly. Their appearance seemed to go unnoticed by all within the establishment as no one looked up or became distracted from their entertainment.

'Keep an eye on him. Let me know when he is finished, but don't let him leave. If I'm right about this one, he is going to owe me one heck of a favour. The God of the Underworld will be happy on this eve.'

Chapter 13

Reaghan struggled between the two soldiers as the punches made contact against his jaw. He slumped forward with each blow to his stomach and could see the blood dripping from his mouth to the floor as if in slow motion. His vision was beginning to swim.

'Reaghan, who would have known your lust was for blood not merely rutting.' Dominic walked around the Chieftain's son with his hands behind his back. 'What am I going to do with you?'

The centurion walked over to the girl cowering in the corner, trying to hide her naked body below the soft cushions that she frantically tried to rearrange. The room was draped with sheer fabric of every colour of the rainbow and the walls were alight with candles, casting dancing shadows around the walls.

'You're going to be alright Antonia. I'm so sorry about Deidre.' Dominic looked at the golden-haired girl whose blue eyes looked vacantly at the ceiling. The blood splattered around the room appeared to have fallen in a pre-ordered pattern. The large pool of crimson that ran from Deidre's belly had begun to congeal and the soldier shook his head. He had expected this, but he was not entirely prepared for the level of carnage.

'Where is Meredith?' Dominic knelt next to Antonia and spoke softly being careful not to touch the girl. After what she had endured, she would likely never work again, but it was a small price to pay to get the information he needed from Reaghan.

'She ran Sir. We heard the screams, but you had been clear that we needed to wait.' A soldier answered for the girl, saluting as he spoke.

'She got away!' Dominic's manner unnerved the soldier and he kept his salute in place. 'You had best see to it then man or word will spread like wildfire and your head will roll.' Dominic pointed the soldier to the door. 'Take as many men as you need and offer whatever sum is necessary to keep her quiet. Do you understand?'

'Yes Sir.' The soldier allowed his hand to fall from the salute and hurriedly waved two more soldiers to join him.

The Chieftain's son hung now between the soldiers, his head bobbing up and down as he tried to stay conscious.

Reaghan had heard the exchange. His mind was swimming after yesterday's beating from Culaan and now with another attack from the soldiers, he was feeling like a great fog had settled on his senses. 'What, is…going…on?'

'Well, that's the question isn't it? You murdered a whore, rather viciously I might add and you have no money to make restitution to the establishment and nothing to offer her family in tribute. Add to that, the Empire doesn't look too kindly on outright murder.'

'I, I don't remember anything. What…was in…the ale?' Reaghan stammered over the words. He lifted his head for only a moment and saw the dead whore on the floor, her legs in an unnatural position. He looked to the remaining whore who refused to make eye contact with anything but her feet.

'Apparently blood lust can be like that. Now we can sort this out, us being friends and all but if your father finds out about what you have done I think he might put you to death himself. Am I right?' Dominic tried unsuccessfully to keep the smile from his lips but Reaghan could barely see past the dead woman in front of him.

'Don't tell him, please!' Reaghan tried not to beg as the centurion's threats began to make sense to him.

'It's going to be very costly Reaghan, keeping the surviving girls quiet and then there's the establishment. They will want a lot of coin.'

'You know I have nothing.' Reaghan now began to understand his mistake.

'Oh, I am sure we can come up with something. Let's say I needed some information? You could help me with that, couldn't you?' Dominic was having so much fun. Working his plans to fruition was like winning a battle but there were no casualties. Well not many he realised as he gazed at the dead girl. He stifled a giggle of excitement.

'What do you want?' Reaghan looked up through his blurred vision, a sense of defeat easily seen in his posture.

'A soldier was killed by a whore recently. Except it turns out that she wasn't really a whore. She wore a long green dress and her hair was dark, like Antonia's here.' Dominic pointed to the whore who began to cry at the attention. 'Get her out of here and clean her up.' He pointed to a soldier by the door.

'Yes Sir.' The soldier saluted and tried to grab the girl by the arm. She screamed at his touch and the soldier looked to Dominic for guidance.

The Officer said nothing, instead he pulled his dagger from his leather kilt and knelt next to Antonia. 'Shut up or die. Now go with Julius here and keep your mouth shut. You understand me!'

The girl nodded and whimpered as Julius gently lifted her by her arm and guided her out of the room.

'Now where were we? That's right. Foreign girl. Long dress. Dead soldier. What do you know?'

Reaghan shook his head as if the action would help him think clearly. 'How did the soldier die?'

'With his own dagger.' Dominic answered flatly.

'A foreign girl who can overpower a soldier of the Empire you say?' Reaghan's head was beginning to clear.

'Yes! You dumb Gaul, that's what I said isn't it?'

'I might have an idea. We have a stranger in the village who is good at attacking men with their own weapon.'

'Sounds promising. What's her name?'

'No idea. I didn't get the chance to ask her.' Reaghan was feeling bold as it became obvious what Dominic wanted.

'The village you say? Best we go take a look. When Julius is finished with the girl, get him to clean up our friend Reaghan here and will someone please clear the room? Keep it quiet now men. Not a word to anyone.'

The soldiers looked at each other and let Reaghan go. He slumped to the floor and peered at the dead woman as tears sprung to his eyes. 'Why did I do that?' He spoke softly, his mind full of confusion.

Dominic left Reaghan with his men. His mind was racing with matters he needed to attend to. He caught sight of the Manager as he left the rear of the establishment.

'Titus, thank you again for your aid. Where on earth did you get that hallucinogenic man?'

The Manager smiled. 'From the Druids believe it or not.'

'Oh, that's precious. Maybe we should think twice about killing that sort of knowledge. I'm sorry about Deidre, really. I had expected him to prefer his own kind, but Meredith would have been a more tolerable loss.'

'True words my friend. Meredith has run off the boys say.'

'Yes, if you see her, keep her quiet won't you? This has gone very nicely and the Senator has put a lot of pressure on me to find Marcellus's killer so let's keep this under wraps as long as possible.'

'It's likely to come out eventually you know.'

'Yes, I don't give a fig if Reaghan ends up dead later, but for now he will prove very helpful. We find this foreign girl, make sure the Senator has his revenge and then we find the rest of the Druids. Their fairy tales of magic are undermining the strength of the Empire and the Emperor has had enough. Time to bring Galatia fully under our control.'

'Couldn't agree more Dominic. You can count on me.' The Manager smiled as the Roman Officer dropped a bulging pouch of gold coins on his counter top. He fought the urge to touch them immediately and Dominic smiled his understanding.

Chapter 14

'So, you came here with the Angel Raziel to avoid a royal wedding?'

'It's more than that Morrigan. I have trained all my life to be a Priestess, to use the gifts God has given me to fight against those who oppose God. In my culture, if I married, then I would have to leave the Order and my training behind. I would never use a bow, swing a sword or summon my gifts again.'

Morrigan patted the Priestess's hand gently. 'It is not so different amongst the Roman culture here child. Women are denied these things, but the Galatians, those descended from the Gauls still allow their women to fight. For that I am thankful.'

'Then that is why I am here, to fight!'

'To fight whom and for what? We don't worship your god Ariela, we have a faith that is as old as your own and we believe in earth magic, something you say is forbidden where you come from.'

'From what I understand of how you have described magic, it is what we call a gift, a gift from God and if the Angel has brought me here, then I am to fight for God.'

'We shall see. Did Raziel tell you anything when he left you here?'

'Nothing, not really anyway. I heard his voice after I arrived. He spoke into my mind, saying he would aid me when needed but he would not reveal himself.'

'Hmm. A god you can't see, Angels that don't materialise and powers you don't call magic. Either way, it seems the Romans are our common enemy. They murdered the man many of your people call the Messiah, the bringer of peace and now they seek to eradicate our faith and our magic. For now, it seems we are on the same side.'

Morrigan moved to the hearth and lifted the boiling pot form the tripod. She used a thick cloth to hold the hot vessel as she poured water into small cups. She placed one on the table before Ariela and carried the other to her seat opposite.

'Drink this.' Morrigan offered.

'What is it?' Ariela sniffed the steam and blinked at the armour.

'It's a herbal tisane. Nothing medicinal, just something to help us both relax. Now tell me about Reaghan and what happened, then maybe I can explain a little more about the local politics.'

Ariela smiled and began to recount her meeting with the Chieftain's son.

A commotion outside the cottage filtered to the two women and Morrigan stood to investigate. As she opened the door Dorran's face greeted her with a wide smile.

'Wise one.' He bowed reverently.

'Dorran, what can I do for you today? Is your wife with child again?'

'No Morrigan. I'm here on the Chieftain's business. I hear we have a visitor in the village.' Dorran peered discretely over the old woman's shoulder. 'Owyn would like very much to meet her.'

'Oh would he now? Can you assure me of her safety Dorran?'

'You have my word Wise One.' The man bowed once more, a permanent grin on his features.

'Stop calling me that. You know how much I hate it when you do that.' Morrigan smiled good-naturedly and turned to Ariela who had stood and moved away from the table.

'Ariela it will be alright.' The Priestess frowned, unconvinced by the wise woman's words. 'I will come with you. Owyn is the Chieftain of this village and many more. The Clan is under his control and protection.' Morrigan spoke smoothly trying to reassure the Priestess it was safe.

'What if I don't choose to go?'

Dorran interrupted. 'That is your right lass, but it would be considered bad manners. The Chieftain has offered you safe passage to meet with him and I guarantee that with my own life.'

Ariela studied the man. His energy was calm and reassuring and his aura was pure with soft blue, reinforcing the truth of his words. His smile was genuine and his eyes reassuringly strong.

'Very well. Shall we go Morrigan?' Ariela collected her new hooded robe and moved past the Druid out into the clearing before the cottage. She caught the eye of Culaan as she joined the men that had accompanied Dorran.

'Can you ride lass?' Dorran asked as he surveyed the villagers milling around wondering what was happening.

'I can. Thank you.' Dorran led a spare mount over to the Priestess who held out her hand in greeting. The animal pranced a moment before it calmed with Ariela's touch. She stroked its mane and moved up alongside to mount up. She did not notice Culaan and Genevieve had moved out from the Huntress's hut to see what all the commotion was about.

'You have a way with the animal lass.' Dorran smiled as he mounted his horse with unexpected agility. He saw Culaan moving closer from the corner of his eye. The lad made no move to interfere, he simply looked to be surveying the group. He carried no weapon and his companion was not armed with her usual bow. Dorran relaxed and returned his attention to his charge.

'Ride with me Morrigan, I know how much you hate to ride on horseback but we need to get to the hall before nightfall.'

Dorran held out his hand to the Druid who hoisted herself effortlessly to the horse's back. Morrigan moved with the grace that belied her age and Ariela raised an eyebrow in surprise.

'Ah sprite as always Wise One.' Morrigan slapped Dorran on the back as she settled in for the ride. She caught sight of Culaan as they rode out but shook her head gently at his concerned eyes.

Ariela looked over her shoulder to Culaan before trotting out of the village relishing the freedom and power of the mount below her. 'At least this hasn't changed, hey boy.' She spoke softly as she stroked the horse's neck. As they cleared the village, she pushed the horse into a canter to keep pace with Dorran and his men.

****

'We need to follow them.' Culaan ignored Morrigan's warning as he watched the horses leave the village. His posture was tense and his eyes remained on the retreating group until they were finally out of view.

'Oh you really like this one, don't you!' Culaan looked defiantly at his friend but said nothing. 'On what are we supposed to follow?' Genevieve held her hands in the air for an answer.

'Horses of course.' Culaan smiled wickedly and relaxed once more.

'Oh no! I have a really bad feeling about this Culaan. Stealing horses carries a severe punishment, death if I recall. Even you can't avoid Clan law.'

'Who said anything about stealing. We will simply borrow them. As long as they are back before the morning, no one will notice.' Culaan started to move away from the village square. He walked to the Huntress's hut and surveyed his weapons. He touched his longsword, before choosing his short-bladed weapon.

He sheathed the short sword and threw Genevieve her quiver and bow.

'No, no, no, no, no.' Genie said the words as she swung her bow and quiver over her shoulder and followed Culaan. As they arrived at the Tavern stables, realisation hit the Huntress. 'Merchants' mounts? Are you out of your mind? No scratch that, of course you are.'

'I told you, no one will notice as long as we get them back before the merchants prepare to leave in the morning. It will be fine, stop worrying. You know you worry too much.' Culaan coaxed Genie through the stable entrance with a quick shove in her back. Her quiver clattered with the sudden movement.

'I don't know how you get me into these situations Culaan. If I didn't love you as much as I do, you know I would never follow you around like this.'

Culaan smiled oblivious to the reality of Genevieve's words. 'I love you too Genie and it's because I love you that I can't let you live a boring uneventful life.' Genevieve sighed in resignation, knowing he would never understand how she felt about him.

'True, life is never dull around you.' She shrugged off her emotions. 'Alright, let's get this over with before I change my mind.' Genevieve pulled a small mountain pony from the stalls and threw a rug over its back before adding a bridle and bit.

Culaan did the same to a grey Persian beast that stood a good two hands taller than the pony. He grinned to his friend as he prepared the mount.

'I think you might be over compensating.' She raised her eyebrows mockingly as she swung up onto the animal and hastily nudged the animal out of the stables before her friend could retaliate.

Culaan watched her move away and mounted his horse to follow, a frown crossed his face momentarily as he considered her words, before he smiled and shook the thought aside.

Chapter 15

'Where are you from lass?' Dorran asked as he moved his mount alongside Ariela's. They were travelling through the dimly lit forest and Dorran moved closer to his charge, wanting to watch her closely.

'Best we leave that for Owyn, Dorran. It is a long tale to be sure.' Morrigan reassured the wily soldier with a smile.

'How long have you served the Chieftain?' Ariela changed the subject with ease as they cantered gently along the well-worn trail.

'Since we were lads. Owyn's family have ruled the Tectosagii clan for generations; since before the peace treaty and the battle of Olympus. My family has served as the Chieftain's Generals or as we are better known now, as advisories throughout our history.'

'An honour for your family then?'

'Or a curse!'

Ariela frowned at Dorran's candour and struggled to find words. 'I'm sorry.' Was all she managed as she averted her gaze to her surroundings once more. The sun was getting low and her backside was beginning to ache. She moved slightly to adjust her position, stifling a wince.

'Don't be sorry lass. Yes, it is an honour to serve Owyn. He is a strong and proud leader, but it is a curse to be a leader of any kind during times like this.'

'I thought you were at peace.' Ariela frowned in confusion.

Dorran's laughter rang out and although Morrigan did not join him, she smiled and stifled a chuckle. Ariela looked from one to the other and could sense the rapport between them.

'We have a treaty in place lass. One that allows the Roman's to take what they want, when they want it. It is not the way of our people to sit back and be *ruled* by others.' Dorran's jaw muscle tightened and for the first time since their meeting Ariela could see fire instead of calm in the man's eyes.

'Your words remind me of my Uncle's. He too does not like being subject to any other, unless you count God of course.' Ariela smiled as she thought of David. A sense of melancholy nudged at her but now was not the time to allow it room to grow. She smiled mysteriously to her companions to hide her sudden memories.

'So! Who is your Uncle?' Dorran grinned, knowing he was unlikely to get the answer he wanted.

'All will be revealed soon enough Dorran.' Morrigan interrupted.

'I don't think Owyn will believe me Morrigan. Why should he?' Ariela adjusted her position, this time not because she was uncomfortable, but because of her growing agitation. The horse's ears moved back and he began to prance once more. She made soothing noises and stroked his neck, calming him quickly.

Dorran opened his mouth to speak but stopped as noises came from the road ahead. He frowned as his men were forced to slow. They reigned in their mounts to allow a regiment of Roman centurions to pass.

Dorran was surprised when they slowed to a halt alongside him. A sense of unease washed over him. 'How goes it Commander?' Dorran planted his most peaceful looking expression on his features.

Ariela looked at Dorran and could read the difference in the man. His face said one thing, but his eyes said another and the tension between his shoulders spoke volumes toward filling in any gaps in this unspoken conversation.

'It goes remarkably well Dorran. I see you have apprehended our murderer.'

Dorran resisted the urge to move his hand to the hilt of his sword. Dominic saw the tension and smiled.

'I see you carry a weapon Dorran. I believe that is against the treaty.' Dominic made no effort to keep the patronising tone from his words.

'It is a hunting weapon only Commander, one to gather food or for protection against beasts if the need arises only.' Dorran puffed his chest up slightly and Morrigan could feel the tension rising between the two leaders.

'Murderer! Whatever do you mean Commander?' Morrigan spoke up from behind the Clansman, hoping to ease the tension with distraction.

'This young woman here.' Dominic lifted his sword from the scabbard at his side as he spoke, the sound grating on everyone with the slow and meticulous manner the Commander employed. 'She killed one of our own not more than one night past and his uncle is most upset.'

'I think you must be mistaken Commander.' Morrigan continued politely.

'Well that is possible, but unlikely. She matches the description perfectly. In fact, she was seen leaving with a woman that looked remarkably like you. Who did you say you were?' The Commander eyed Ariela and smirked.

'I could be wrong about you of course, but this one,' Dominic pointed his finger at Ariela, 'she is definitely the girl we seek. You don't see too many foreigners around here. Now I don't want to upset the Clan for now, I just need the girl to come with me and the rest of you can leave quietly.' The threat was not lost on the Priestess. If she didn't give herself up, Morrigan would be arrested with her.

'I am sure this is all simply a misunderstanding.' Ariela spoke with great care, keeping her tone polite and neutral. 'It is alright Dorran.' The man's hand had drifted close to his weapon. 'You can speak with Owyn on my behalf and I am sure I can help this man see I am not the person he is looking for.'

Morrigan looked into Ariela's eyes and saw a calmness she didn't feel herself. 'Is there anything I can do for you lass?'

'I am sure you can cook something up for me.' Ariela didn't use the Druid's name, she didn't want to betray her to the Roman. 'You have such a talent with herbs, everything you make tastes delicious. I will be back before you know it. I'm sure.' Morrigan frowned for only a moment before realisation struck. She nodded her understanding.

'Splendid. Now toss me those reins girl and we can be on our way.' Dominic motioned for Ariela to move closer. He took the reins from her hands almost gently and pulled out a leather rope, which he bound around her wrists not so gently. 'You can't be too careful with murderers you know.' He smiled brightly, looking the Priestess in the eyes.

'I am a suspect, am I not? Don't you have a royal court or someone with the anointed power to adjudicate in such matters?'

Dominic smiled. 'Of course we do girl. He is the Uncle of the soldier you killed. Your trial will be swift and your punishment long and painful.'

Dorran moved to intercede, but Morrigan put her hand on his shoulder. 'I gave my word no harm would come to her Morrigan. I must honour my word.' He whispered over his shoulder.

'You will my friend, you will. Take me to Owyn, now!'

****

Culaan had heard the large troop of horses moving before Dorran's men were intercepted. He and Genevieve had circled around carefully, leading their horses so as not to be heard.

Now as they watched the exchange, the young clansman's blood began to boil. 'How can Dorran let her be taken like that?'

'What do you suggest he do with a short hunting knife, throw it!' Genevieve tried to keep her sarcasm under control but Culaan could be so single minded and stupid at times.

'The damned treaty, forbidding us from carrying decent weapons. Reaghan seems to get away with it Why is that?' Culaan looked at his short sword. 'I knew I should have brought my longsword.'

'We still have this!' Genevieve raised her bow with a smile.

'Thank the goddess for hunting bows.' Culaan smiled and then looked at the size of the regiment that accompanied Ariela as they rode away from Dorran.

'There are too many for one short sword and a bow.' The Romans disappeared from their view as Culaan and Genevieve moved into the open, their horses still trailing behind them.

Dorran turned his mount to the sound of voices on their flank, his short sword drawn this time without any hesitation.

'I told you not to follow Culaan.' The Druid was frowning.

'Yes, but luckily I don't do everything you tell me to do. What is going on?'

'Dominic has arrested Ariela for killing someone's nephew.' Dorran sheathed his sword as he spoke.

'What!'

'I will explain on the way. We need to get to your father.' Morrigan interrupted.

'Why?' Culaan began to mount his horse once more.

'Just follow Culaan and for once in your young head-strong life, just do as the old Wise One tells you.' Dorran kept his tone calm.

'Lucky for you old friend that I value your counsel as much as my father.' Culaan turned his horse as he mounted and trotted over to Dorran. 'It is good to see you.' They clasped arms in the warriors' greeting and Dorran patted the younger man on the back.

'When you two are finished getting reacquainted, do you think we can go? I gauge we have very little time before they execute Ariela. Dominic's reputation precedes him and Ariela will no doubt endure one of his infamous interrogations before the Senator even sees her.' Morrigan saw the fear touch Culaan's eyes. He began to move out, turning for a moment to ensure that Genevieve would follow.

She nodded her agreement and pushed her mount forward as the group moved off toward Ankyra and Owyn.

Chapter 16

'What do you want me to do Morrigan? I have to consider the safety of all of our people...a foreigner or all of us! You really want me to choose her?' The Chieftain sat tensely as he looked down on his kin.

'It isn't as if we didn't know this time would come Owyn. Our people are not made to be held prisoner to another man's yoke.' Morrigan stood with her hands on her hips, Dorran at her side amongst the Chieftain's other counsellors.

Culaan watched the exchange and his discomfort continued to escalate. Genevieve placed her hand on his arm in understanding as he resisted the urge to pace. 'We are wasting time.' He hissed quietly.

'This is Owyn we're talking about.' Genevieve shrugged. 'And he is right in our way.' The Huntress grimaced knowing her words would not land gently. Culaan scowled at her remark and she shrugged her apology.

'What do you propose Morrigan? Should we launch a full-scale attack on a full regiment of the Roman centurions? How do you believe that will turn out?'

'Don't be so facetious Owyn. We lost thousands to the Romans last time we attacked head on. I remember it as though it were yesterday.' The Druid took a deep breath to calm the images that forced their way back into her mind.

Owyn saw the Druid's face grow pale. 'I spoke hastily. Sometimes I forget who you truly are Morrigan and I should heed your counsel for that is the role of the Druid, but much has changed.' The Chieftain stood up from his chair and paced the dais.

'Yes, but we still have magic, at least for now Owyn.' Morrigan put up her hand before the Chieftain could object. 'Your lack of faith isn't unique but it is disappointing and it drains the gods of their power.'

Culaan couldn't contain himself any longer. He pushed his way to the front of the hall, past the soldiers who hid behind the guise of the Chieftain's counsel and up to his father's throne as he considered it.

'What magic Morrigan? What are you talking about?' Culaan reached the Druid and stood towering over her, his broad shoulders heaving with chained power and frustration.

'Ariela is not what you believe. She spoke of her history to you Culaan.'

'Yes, she sounded delusional with talk of the ancient Israelites and Kings of old. It was strange.'

'It was entirely true.' Morrigan turned back to Owyn. 'Ariela is not from this place, that you know, but she is the answer to many Druid prayers. I assure you.'

Morrigan warned Culaan with a frown not to expand on Ariela's story and the young warrior chose to keep quiet, at least for now. He raised an eyebrow in Genevieve's direction and smiled at the thought of anything Ariela had said being even remotely true.

'She spoke in riddles when we left her.' Dorran looked up at Owyn as he spoke, then turned to Morrigan. 'Why did she leave so calmly?'

'Because she asked me for help and I will give it to her.'

'I told you Morrigan, we can't fight the Romans.' Owyn moved down a step from the platform toward the Druid in frustration.

'Who said anything about fighting? All I need is a distraction. Do you think you can manage a little commotion in the Roman camp Owyn?'

The Chieftain smiled as he moved alongside his visitors. 'What do you have in mind?'

Morrigan outlined her plan as Dorran removed his short sword and replaced it with his longsword scabbard.

****

Ariela made no sound as the soldiers dragged her down into the lower level of the estate. Instead, she held her head high and watched her surroundings carefully. The halls were narrow and dark, with only the occasional wall torch lit. There were no windows in any of the rooms and little or no furniture.

The soldiers placed her wrists in metal shackles on the wall and stepped back from the room as the Commander entered.

'That will be all now men. Leave the lower level entirely. This one is for me and me alone. I don't require an audience.' Dominic motioned for his men to leave the room and Ariela couldn't help but notice the disappointment on the soldiers' faces.

Dominic moved closer to the Priestess until she was staring into his now glazed over eyes. She fought the first pangs of fear by closing her eyes momentarily in prayer. The Centurion laughed at what he thought was her fear of him and reached out to touch her.

'You are a pretty morsel to behold.' Dominic studied the girl's bronze skin and dark, thick hair of ringlets. She was alluring and he brushed his face against her cheek so he could take in the scent of her hair. 'I am curious, how does a slight little girl like you overpower a soldier like Marcellus?'

'Was that his name?' Ariela opened her eyes and smiled sweetly. 'I wish I had met him, he must have been a special person for your Senator to be so angered that he would seek out any young woman to blame for his death.'

The Priestess made no move to shy away from her captor. There was nowhere to run, her back was hard against the wall and she was determined to stay strong.

Ariela stared defiantly into Dominic's eyes as he pushed her even harder into the stone wall of her prison. Instead of crying or complaining, the young girl only goaded the Centurion. 'Tell me, why is it that this

Marcellus you speak of was alone with a young woman who would wish to kill him?'

The cold jagged edges of the stone bit into Ariela's back and legs as the Commander rubbed his body up against her thin tunic. Stripped now of her woollen cloak, the Priestess tried not to shiver from the cold.

'Let me set you straight girl.' Dominic supressed the urge to lick the foreigners soft tanned face. 'My superior is a Senator of the Roman Empire and his nephew was high born, so, how should I put this…' Dominic licked his lips and smirked in a way that failed to reach his eyes… 'Marcellus had the right to do almost anything he wanted to — except die.'

Ariela could feel the soldier's arousal and she forced herself to remain calm. She did not struggle in the bindings that held her hands, instead she opened her hips to the soldier, offering herself willingly.

'I see why Marcellus was distracted but there is no weapon for you to use against me whore. I didn't miss the fact that Marcellus died by his own blade and although I know you are unarmed,' Dominic slid his hand beneath the Priestess's tunic. 'it is always worth checking.'

The Commander smiled as he forced the girl's legs apart and began to unclasp his leather kilt. Ariela waited patiently, ignoring the bile rising in her throat.

****

Culaan tied the knife onto Genevieve's leg as he spoke. She looked at him and wondered if he even realised her leg was bare. 'Be careful Genie.' He touched her hand as he stood and she brushed her dress into place.

'Why? Do I detect a hint of worry?' Genevieve continued to prepare her appearance.

'Don't get used to it.' Culaan nodded as the Huntress moved into the courtyard.

Genevieve hadn't played the alluring female in some time. With her golden hair and light speckling of freckles she was never considered stunning, but she knew she was attractive enough to do what needed to be done.

She looked down at her bulging bosom and smiled. It was a significant change from her woollen tunic and long leather woodsman's boots; the thought invoked a mischievous grin and Genevieve looked back over her shoulder as she adjusted her cleavage with both hands. Culaan rolled his eyes and Genevieve stifled a giggle.

She blew him a kiss and began the walk across the courtyard toward the Senator's estate. The night was cool with a clear sky, thousands of stars and only a sliver of moon for light.

The walls of the estate came into view within moments and the Huntress touched the concealed knife gently for reassurance.

'Lads. It's a rather lovely night out isn't it?' The Huntress watched the small gathering of guards outside the private residence. 'Is the Lord of the manor home tonight? Could he do with a little companionship?'

A short and stout Officer moved forward. 'Move along whore. The Senator has no need of cheap and common sluts to warm his bed.'

'Well maybe your friends there might like a little distraction from their boring work.' Genevieve nodded at the young soldiers behind the Officer and he smiled at the idea.

'How much?' Two more soldiers moved forward to listen to the cost. Both eyed Genevieve's cleavage admiringly.

'A copper each, but one at a time lads. You should savour the moment. It's a numbers game you see. I wouldn't normally be so cheap but let's just say I'm offering a bulk deal tonight.'

The men looked at each other and smiled. 'You're a pretty clean whore for a copper each.' The Officer asked, still curious. The Huntress pushed up her bosom to help seal the deal while she carefully considered their weapons.

'Do you think you can all be patient and wait your turn lads?' Genevieve smiled as the men nodded their agreement, including the Officer. 'Who goes first then?'

The Officer moved forward and grabbed the Huntress around the waist. 'Over here girl.' He rubbed his body against Genevieve's hip as he circled her into his arms, leading her to the alley adjacent to the entrance.

The alley was lined with high buildings on either side and the lack of moonlight left them both in near pitch darkness. 'I wouldn't mind getting my hands on you in better lighting. I have a hunch you are a sight to behold. But they say it's all in the tasting, not the seeing after all.'

The Officer began to unlace Genevieve's dress, rubbing his face in her cleavage as he fumbled with the bodice laces. The Huntress reached into a hidden pocket, finding her weapon of choice and waited for the soldier to lift his head.

The man took longer than she had hoped before he lifted his head, cupping her breast in his hand and smiling stupidly. The Huntress placed the fine powder from her pocket onto her palm and blew it into the soldier's face not unlike blowing him a kiss. She held her breath so as not to inhale any herself while the soldier smirked before he began to feel the effects.

His eyes grew wide and the pupils became dilated almost instantly. Genevieve almost giggled as the soldier's hands dropped to his side and he looked vacantly into her eyes. 'Moan like you are rutting the sexiest woman alive.'

'You are such a cruel woman. Remind me to never get on your bad side.' Culaan walked up behind Genevieve as he spoke. The Officer had begun to moan as ordered. Genevieve tucked herself back in and began to tie up her bodice.

'This is amazing. I will have to keep some of this for personal use. Are you seeing this?' The man began to moan louder and for a moment the Huntress was worried he might reach a climax. Her thoughts were interrupted as Morrigan joined them.

'I don't think so lass. I will search you thoroughly before we leave here.' Morrigan smiled at the scene before her. 'It is very effective though, isn't it?'

'You too are both very cruel you know.' Culaan almost felt sorry for the man. 'He is going to feel very unfulfilled after this.'

Both women giggled softly as Culaan shook his head.

'What now?' Genevieve looked to Morrigan for instructions.

'Now we repeat the process. Tell your friend there to go get the next soldier and then fall asleep by the fire. Don't forget to ask him to tell his friends just how great you were.'

'I like the way you think Morrigan.' Genevieve moved to the soldier and whispered in his ear. 'Now you had all better get ready. We move as soon as the last soldier has been serviced.' The Huntress chuckled to herself as she moved the soldier out of the darkness, her arm wrapped in his as though they were a courting couple

'What is that powder Morrigan?' Culaan whispered to the Druid as he watched the sway of Genevieve's hips in the familiar dark green dress she now wore as she moved into the light of the courtyard.

'Devil's Breath. It is a plant extract. When you treat is just right, it can make almost anyone obey your every command.'

'I think I could use a little of that myself.'

'You don't need Devil's Breath to get what you want Culaan.' Morrigan patted him on the cheek as his eyes continued to linger on the retreating Huntress. 'You simply have to make up your mind what it is you really desire most.'

Chapter 17

The Ortagion tavern was humming with activity as Dorran and his men sauntered in. The main bar room was almost evenly divided like the sides of a stadium full of Gladiators.

The Roman soldiers mingled to one end of the bar, filtering deeper into the tavern where a game of knuckle bones was eliciting a loud round of betting. The Clansmen occupied the other end of the bar and the unspoken space between the two groups was not wide, but it may as well have been a canyon.

Dorran pointed to a small group of his men and nodded that they should join in with the knuckle bone betting.

Two more of his men were directed to the Clansmen who mingled with other Galatian residents, and set about their work. Dorran tapped his foot irritably as he considered the plan.

The tavern was poorly lit and Dorran squinted to keep an eye on everyone, cursing his aging eyes.

'Honey. Can I get you a drink of something?' A short and stout woman called to Dorran over the heads of rows of men who blocked his way to the long wooden bar.

'Don't mind if I do lass.' Dorran grinned good naturedly and wove his way to the front. The bar was covered in spilt ale and a long linen fabric with the Tectosagii Clan colours adorned the counter top. He took a moment to admire the barmaid and judged her in her early forties with overly large breasts and broad hips that only added to his admiration.

'Lass!' The woman laughed loudly. 'You are a funny one. I'm long past lass, but I will take the compliment in any case.' Dorran reached out to accept the tall clay jug of amber liquid and took a long gulp of it before setting it down.

'You are a bonnie lass to an old timer like me.' The smile reached his eyes and they glistened with appreciation.

'Are you flirting with me?' The woman batted her eyelashes too easily and Dorran stifled a chuckle.

'Aye, flirting, but I am a married man and although my eye might rove, I never follow through lass.' Dorran lifted the jug in salute and tossed a copper to the woman. 'Thank you for the drink.' He turned and moved from the bar, making his way towards a table by the window. It was well lit with candles and less populated.

A crash alerted the old warrior, who ducked as a heavy wooden bench flew past his face, narrowly missing him as he stepped aside to avoid tripping over the obstacle. He ignored the commotion, instead he moved casually toward the window, took a seat, moved the candle on the table to the windowsill and lifted his drink to his lips for another swig.

Culaan saw the signal from the building across the road and turned to leave. The sound of cracking timber made him swing back around in time to see a young broad shouldered Clansman with plaited blonde hair fly high into the air, landing heavily on the hard-packed earth outside the tavern.

The warrior smiled as he made his way back to Morrigan. His broadsword was sheathed on his back and the dagger at his side beckoned him. He fidgeted with the weapon as he ran through the dark alley, past the courtyard and back to the Senator's residence.

He moved past the unconscious guards and into the Senator's yard. The residence was two storeys of solid stone. There was a long balcony adorned with intricate metal railing and arched openings that ran all the way along the front of the mansion.

As he approached the front entrance, he saw a dead soldier on the ground, an arrow protruding from his neck. He looked around to see if he could spot Genevieve, but couldn't, she was well hidden.

He drew his blade and entered the grand entrance. The stairs drew upwards before him in a spiral going up to the next floor. There was a sliver of light being cast from a room at the top of the stairs, but otherwise the top floor looked empty.

Behind the spiral staircase, he saw a doorway leading to the storeroom below. The light flowed brightly from this door and Culaan could hear faint noises floating up the stone stairs as he opened the heavy wooden door.

He took a deep breath, drew his dagger and started down the narrow stone stairwell into the long hallway below.

****

Ariela calmed her breathing and focussed her energy. Small and almost invisible sparks ignited and faded as Ariela made tiny circles with her fingers. Dominic had dropped his leather kilt to the floor and began shoving the Priestess's dress up around her waist with renewed frenzy.

'I am a Priestess. I warn you. To violate a Priestess of the Order of Shiloh is to bring the wrath of the God of Israel.' Dominic stopped and faced Ariela, eye to eye. His breath was hot on her skin. For a fleeting moment she thought her words had reached him but then he roughly shoved her around to face the stone and lifted her hips with both his hands.

The shaft of light didn't reach its target but the sound it made when it exploded against the table on the far wall was all the distraction she needed. As Dominic spun round to find the cause, Ariela turned and brought her knee into the soldier's encouraged groin. The groan was loud and as he dropped his head to clasp his manhood, Ariela brought her knee up to meet his face.

Dominic dropped to the stone floor, his knees hitting the hard surface, his face ashen with pain, his lips moving wordlessly.

The Priestess grabbed her shackles with both her hands and supported her weight as she lifted her legs and placed them tightly round the Roman soldier's neck. He struggled as the air ceased to enter his lungs and his eyes bulged with sudden fear. He clawed at Ariela's legs but she only squeezed tighter.

The Priestess ignored the sounds erupting from the hallway and failed to notice Culaan reach the doorway to her cell. He stood motionless as he heard the gut wrenching crack of Dominic's neck and the body fall lifeless to the floor.

Ariela looked up as movement caught her eye. Culaan looked from her to the dead soldier and back again, then without a word he moved to the Priestess's side and began unpinning her shackles.

'Remind me never to annoy you.' Was all he said as the shackles dropped free of Ariela's wrists.

'Too late for that.' The Priestess smiled then nodded past Culaan toward two soldiers who now appeared at the entrance to the cell.

Culaan drew his dagger and swung around to face the next challenge. 'I thought Genevieve had us covered?'

Ariela moved wide, warily seeking out Dominic's weapon. He had wisely not been carrying it, but it had to be there somewhere. She scanned the room with her eyes before she noticed a mounted short sword behind what was left of the Commander's desk. 'Best we find her then, before they bring reinforcements.'

Culaan watched Ariela move toward the mounted weapon and knew he needed to give her space to reach it.'

'Alright lads. The lass has been through enough and we can't leave witnesses. Come before the rightful Lord of this land and die by my sword.' The men snarled at the brazen disregard for their power in the region and Culaan grinned as they both charged him.

Ariela didn't waste a moment. She skirted round the two soldiers as Culaan engaged them. The first; a stout man with dark skin and a hooked nose took a kick to his stomach before he could bring his weapon to bear. The second was more cunning and moved wide to Culaan's left, trying to catch him off side, but the young Clansman tossed his sword to his left hand and ably met the clumsy charge.

Ariela pulled the short sword clear of the wall and turned to see the first soldier recovered his footing. 'Over here! Can't you take a woman in a fair fight?'

The soldier saw his friend fighting back at the lightning speed attack from the clansman, but he couldn't leave Ariela on his flank unattended even if he wasn't convinced she had the ability to do any harm. He looked from Ariela to his comrade and back before his decision was made.

He ran at Ariela, a scream of rage meant to frighten her rang out. The Priestess smiled and spun the short sword around with precision. The soldier realised his mistake too late, as Ariela moved gracefully aside, allowing the man's forward movement to throw him off balance, while she delicately spun like a dancer, her sword slicing through soft neck tissue and producing a fine cut through the soldier's jugular.

Culaan switched his sword back to his dominant hand and quickly dispatched his opponent with an upward thrust to the heart. The man's eyes glazed over before he reached the ground.

'You are full of surprises aren't you?' Culaan pointed to the exit as he spoke. 'Let's move. Genevieve should have handled all the others by now, but our distraction won't last for ever.'

'What about the Senator?'

'I don't think he is home. Besides, we leave the Senator alone. For now!' Culaan nodded for her to move.

Chapter 18

There were Roman soldiers and Clansmen scattered throughout the tavern when Owyn arrived. 'What is the meaning of this?' he roared as he entered the dimly lit room. Lanterns had fallen and candles were scattered, but the sun would be rising soon and the Chieftain could see the damage was extensive.

'You have my sincere apology Nexus. I'll see to it that each man who participated is punished and we will all help put your establishment back to rights.'

The overweight and red-faced owner wiped his hands on his stained apron and tried to be convincing. 'I try to run a fair tavern here lads. All men are equals when they walk through those doors over there.' The man pointed to the entrance. 'Now, the next man that starts a fight in here on either side, will get a flogging. Do you understand?'

The Clansmen were lined up like children, with their bloodied heads hanging low and their clothing dishevelled.

'I'm not sure that will do Owyn.' The Senator stepped forward with his hands on his hips and his chest puffed out with exaggerated importance. His men were not lined up shamelessly, they were being attended to by the Roman physicians as barmaids scurried about serving food to those not wounded.

'A vicious attack took place in the basement of my residence last night while all this was going on.' The Senator swept his hand around the mess of broken tables and debris.

'I am sorry to hear that my Lord, but my men it seems were too busy embarrassing their fellow clansmen to know anything about such a travesty.' Owyn kept his face even. 'I will investigate the incident though, you have my word Senator.'

The Senator studied the Chieftain carefully, trying to read his expression. 'Your men started this fight.' He allowed the accusation to weigh heavily for a moment. 'I'm not sure you know nothing of this incident.'

Owyn smiled amicably. 'I have no doubt my men started the fight Senator. It appears they also finished it.' The Chieftain put his hand up when his men began to cheer. 'But we know nothing of your misfortune. Nexus and his staff can vouch for that, even your own men should be able to confirm this.'

The Senator looked to his soldiers and his shoulders sank. 'My Commander is dead. My nephew is dead and my men live because...'

'My men were unarmed.' Owyn finished. 'I understand Senator. It should not have happened and I assure you, it won't happen again. Dorran, get these men home to their families and prepare teams of six to return every four hours to help put the Ortagion back to rights.'

'Yes Sir.' Dorran began barking commands to the clansmen who slowly made their way out of the tavern towards their respective homes.

'May I ask Senator?' The Roman looked at Owyn with a frown. 'What happened in your basement last evening?' The Chieftain knew he was pushing his luck, but the cringing look on the Senator's face was worth the risk.

****

Owyn returned with Dorran and the men seemed cheerful, even mildly elated. Many had returned to their families but a handful had joined their Chieftain in the hall. They celebrated amongst the memories of their ancestors, the sense of celebration after their small victory returning some sense of honour to the Clan once more.

Morrigan appeared amused at their childish revelling while Culaan kept his distance, sitting in the shadows at the far end of the long table, mulling over the evening's events in private.

The hall was alight with wall-mounted lanterns as the tall narrow windows were beginning to show the signs of dawn. The walls were lined with shields and weapons of war that were no longer allowed to be anything other than decorations.

The Chieftain made his way to the large fur-lined chair on the raised wooden platform and sank down as Dorran took a seat alongside him.

'What now?' Ariela whispered to Genevieve. Both young women had found a quiet spot on an old and gnarled wooden bench to the side of the hall.

'Now we hope that Rome doesn't send someone to replace our Senator.'

Ariela looked confused and opened her mouth to ask more.

'So! This is the mysterious girl of Israel you spoke of Morrigan?' All heads turned and all eyes fell to the Priestess sitting quietly trying to remain unnoticed. Ariela looked from Genevieve to the Chieftain and frowned.

'He is harmless Ariela.' Genevieve lent over and assured her with a whisper in her ear.

Ariela straightened in her seat but said nothing. Instead she looked to Morrigan for the answer to the question that had been squarely directed to the Druid as though Ariela were mute. She resisted the urge to speak and Owyn chuckled at her obvious restraint.

'Owyn, I apologise. I should have introduced you already. This is Ariela. Priestess of the Order of Shiloh.' Owyn raised an eyebrow at the name of the Order. 'Niece to King David and daughter to the Order's founding Priestess, Nina.'

Owyn stood and bowed to Ariela. The Priestess raised her eyebrows in surprise. 'You come from a prestigious line Priestess but one that died out centuries ago. How do you explain this phenomenon?'

Ariela waited, digesting the Galatian clansman's reverent manner and the significance of the question. She looked to Morrigan for guidance but the old Druid

merely shrugged. The Priestess stood and moved toward
the platform, not taking her eyes from the Chieftain's
face. 'If I tried to explain it, you might simply believe me
insane or deluded as most have so far.' Ariela caught
Genevieve's eye for only a moment.

'It's been a long time since I have seen the magic
of our people at work Ariela. I thought it all but extinct
but I don't doubt you are who you say you are. You
bested my son and although Reaghan would not speak of
it, others have and we are yet to hear exactly how you
escaped Dominic before Culaan arrived.'

'I hadn't exactly escaped yet your Grace. I was still
shackled when Culaan arrived.'

'Interesting.' Owyn smiled, even more intrigued
by how Dominic had died while the Priestess was still
shackled to a wall.

'I think it might be wise to have this discussion
with your counsel and a small few in attendance Owyn.'
Dorran whispered so only his friend could hear. The
Chieftain nodded his understanding as he looked around
acknowledging his kin still celebrating.

'Let us take this meeting to my home shall we?'
Culaan rose to join his father, as did Genevieve but
Owyn raised his hand to stop them.

Ariela took a deep breath, her decision made.
'Your Grace, I would like Culaan and Genevieve present
if it pleases you. They have been with me and protected
me since I arrived.'

Culaan hid his surprise, while Genevieve smiled
her obvious pleasure. 'Your manners are impeccable
Priestess. Very well, Dorran, bring Morrigan, Culaan,

Genevieve and the rest of my counsel together with our new friend here to my private quarters.'

Dorran rose and lead the small group away while Owyn stood and mingled with his men, shaking hands and patting individuals on the back, exchanging jests and calling each man by name. Ariela watched the man as she left the hall just as Genevieve linked arms with her.

'What are you thinking?' The Huntress asked, a genuine smile of friendship on her lips.

'I was just watching Owyn with his men and he reminds me of my father. His manner with the men is like my father with the Priestesses; familiar, respectful yet strong and ordered.'

'Yes, true. It's a shame he doesn't have the same rapport with his own sons.'

'That doesn't surprise me. My father was distant with me too. I think I understand why now. I wish I could see him again.'

'Why can't you?' Genevieve was confused.

'Because somehow, deep down, I think I knew when I agreed to come here that there would be no going back.'

The small group made their way across the small township that sat on the outskirts of Ankyra. The Chieftain's home was only slightly larger than the other roughly built cabins in the village.

'Why does the Senator live in a mansion while the Chieftain of your entire clan lives in a cottage not much larger than the common folk.' Ariela surveyed the homes as she spoke.

'Our leaders never live higher on the hog than the common folk. That's not how leadership works here.' Genevieve smiled

'Higher on the hog?'

'It's a saying. He doesn't eat a better cut of meat or live a more lavish life than the rest of us. Not like the Roman pigs. They drink from golden goblets while their poor starve. The mansion the Senator lives in belongs to a Roman merchant who is high born and lives in Rome. He leases it out to the Empire for whoever rules in Galatia.'

'This is something my uncle always feared might happen to our people as the wealth grew.'

'I think his fears came to fruition Priestess. Your people gave up their own Prophet to keep the Roman's at bay. They would sell their own mother if they thought there was a gold coin in it or it would keep them safe.'

'You people don't hold anything back do you?' Ariela spoke without anger.

'Who needs to beat around the bush when you can speak plainly?'

'Beat around the bush, high on the hog! It seems I have more than a new language to master here.'

They had reached the Chieftain's home and Culaan opened the door for everyone. 'It's been a while since I set foot in here.' The warrior was sombre, remaining in his own space during the walk.

Genevieve patted him on the shoulder as they entered. Culaan followed, leaving the door open for his father to follow when he was ready.

'Can I get anyone some water?' Dorran moved to a jug on the table.

'I could do with something a little heavier thanks Dorran. Culaan suggested and Morrigan slapped him on the back of the head gently.

'The sun is barely cresting the mountains and already you try to drown your problems with ale.'

Culaan shrugged. 'It's never failed me so far.'

Owyn entered the main room of his home. 'Take a seat if you can find one everyone. It's a little cramped but we should keep Ariela's story between ourselves for now.'

Ariela took the cup of water offered by Dorran and sat where he suggested on a long wooden bench beside the table. Culaan moved to the hearth and lent against the mantel, politely refusing the cup Dorran offered him. Genevieve moved alongside her friend sensing he needed some moral support but unsure exactly how to offer it.

Ariela took a slow and steady breath before she began to explain about the Angel Raziel and how she came to be in this time. The small group listened without interruption and when she finished, Culaan let out a low whistle.

'Now that explains a lot, but raises only more questions. Why?'

'Exactly my question, but Raziel is yet to answer clearly. He only said I would know.' Ariela took a sip of water and placed the cup on the table.

'Well your training is extensive. Maybe we start by learning how you harness your magic?' Owyn smiled.

'You remind me of someone your Grace. My Uncle was very much like you.

'Call me Owyn and I hope it is the King you are referring to. You honour me lass.' Ariela smiled.

'No, not the King. The King's General. Martinez. He married my father's sister, another Priestess of the Order.'

'Ah, I had hoped you meant the King, but come to think of it, his reign has ended and so too has mine, so maybe we are more alike than you believe?'

'No Owyn. Your reign has not yet ended and although David was King, Martinez was loyal, strong and always fair and righteous. A true man of God.'

'Your God has changed colours and stripes over the centuries since your people were here Priestess. The Pharisees and Sadducees fight for power within your faith and now a new religion emerges, one that is said to break with all the traditions of your Torah.'

'The Torah was never my law your Grace, Owyn.' Ariela smiled. 'I am a woman to be bartered for gold and sold into marriage. The Torah is a book written for men, by men. I am a Priestess, yet the Torah has forbidden me from worship within the temple of God and outlawed my use of God's gifts.'

'Ah, then we have common ground. Our Druid magic is forbidden and now the Roman's seeks to stamp out all our kind.'

Ariela felt light-headed and images of her vision returned. She held out her arm to steady herself as her senses were overloaded. The soldiers were running through the village once more. Her hands were glowing with balls of fire and Genevieve's bow was alight with angelic power.

'Ariela, speak to me. Ariela, can you hear me?' Culaan had seen the Priestess sway and even though Genevieve was closer, he had caught her as she fell from the bench to the floor.

Owyn looked to Morrigan and they both smiled. Genevieve knelt beside the young woman and moved her dark hair from her now pale face.

'Do something Morrigan.' Culaan pleaded.

'She is fine Culaan. I can sense her spirit.'

'Ariela.' Culaan continued to shake the Priestess gently.

'I…I, what happened?'

'You tell us lass.' Morrigan moved forward. She gently touched Ariela's hand and a small release of energy sparked loudly enough for all to hear.

'I saw something. It's the second time now.'

Everyone waited patiently. 'There has been no prophecy amongst the Clans for generations.' Morrigan spoke quietly. 'I doubt Culaan or Genevieve have ever heard one uttered. Take your time lass. What did you see?'

'Roman soldiers storming the village and weapons empowered by, by...'

'Magic.' Morrigan finished for her.

'Not the word I would have used, but yes, magic.'

Chapter 19

'I have seen enough of your kin today. Why are you here?' The Senator sipped his watered wine and rearranged the ornaments on his study desk absentmindedly. At least this one wasn't in pieces he mused.

'I am sorry about your loss Senator.' Reaghan tried to appear compassionate.

'Yes, a nasty business. I don't want to think about it.' The image of Dominic on the floor of the cell, his neck broken and his nakedness revealed for all to see returned unbidden.

'It was fortunate you were not in residence at the time.' The Senator nodded but said nothing. 'I hear you lost a prisoner when your Officer was killed.' Reaghan rubbed the soft fabric of the chair and fought to control his emotions.

'Yes, what I would give to find her. She is a witch, of that I am sure.'

'Interesting you should speak of magic and witchcraft. I might be able to help you find the girl.' The

Senator raised an eyebrow questioningly. 'My father knows more than he is letting on.'

'You would give your own father up to see the woman recaptured?' The Senator kept the disdain from his lips. There were times when people like Reaghan could be useful.

'I will give you more than my father. You want to eradicate the magic, the witches, the Druids.' Reaghan waited for added emphasis. 'I know where one is and my father protects them all. Complete folly.'

'Interesting.' The Senator also allowed the silence to grow. The hairs on the back of his neck were standing on end but he pushed the feeling aside and continued negotiations. 'And what do you want in return for this help?' The Senator had a fairly good idea, but he wanted to hear with his own ears.

'It is a lost cause fighting the Empire. You and I both know this. All I want is to take my father's place, my rightful place as leader of our Clan.'

'To what end?'

Reaghan looked confused as he spoke. 'Just to be the Chieftain. What else is there?'

'But you will have no real power. I am the Senator and Rome still rules here.'

'Aye, I see what you mean. I don't seek to displace the Empire. I like your gold too much. You have no need to fear me. My people will continue to be at your service under my rule. I simply want to live a life of luxury, a more Roman lifestyle if you like.'

'Hmmm.' The Senator stood and paced. 'Going up against your father won't be easy and how many more Druids are there hiding in the woodlands.'

'I've not heard of any other wielders of magic and even the one I know has no real power. She crushes herbs and mends broken bones, but there is nothing more to the old folklore than witch woman remedies and old wives' tales.'

'I wish I had your confidence Reaghan, but for now just find out what you can about the girl. Where she is, who is with her and when she is most vulnerable. I will have her head for the death of my nephew and Dominic.'

'As your wish, Senator.' Reaghan rose from his chair and bowed deeply to the Roman Commander. He tried to wipe the smile from his face but failed.

He moved past the guard at the front gates and out into the street. He felt a chill pass over his spine and for a moment, he felt someone might be watching him. He stopped and scanned the surrounding buildings, up the road and behind him until finally he pushed the feeling aside and moved on.

****

'We have a problem Owyn.' Dorran moved into Owyn's quarters uninvited and sat down in the first chair he saw.

'Sounds ominous Dorran, do you think I can get dressed first?' Dorran laughed aloud as he looked up to see Owyn standing before his wash basin, a razor in hand, his face covered in foam and his body naked in every way.

'I apologise for the intrusion. Of course, by all means, finish getting dressed.' There was no embarrassment between the men, but Dorran stepped outside as his friend readied himself. 'I will give you a moment.'

Dorran returned and took the same seat, while Owyn took the one opposite.

'What's going on?' Owyn wiped the remaining shaving foam from his face and tossed the towel aside.

'It's Reaghan. My man followed him. There was a commotion at the whore house, Reaghan left battered and bruised but in one piece.'

'Nothing unusual there. Why the urgency?'

'Dominic and his men were there, before they attacked Ariela.' Owyn groaned but Dorran kept speaking. 'There is more. There are rumours but nothing solid yet. Two whores are missing, both Galatian girls.'

'Send men to find them. Do we have names?'

'Yes, Meredith and Deidre. Neither have family, that's why the Roman's employed them but I might know a way to find them.'

'How?'

'Morrigan.'

'I thought you didn't have time for Druids?' Owyn teased.

'I always have time for Morrigan.' Dorran winked mischievously.

'You must explain your relationship with that woman one day. There is more to it than her delivering your offspring, of that I am sure.'

'Aye I never kiss and tell my friend. You know that.'

'Yet you asked me to hand her over to the Romans.'

'No, I suggested it was a possible way to appease the Empire. I didn't expect you to do it. I'm your advisor. It's my job to advise.'

The mood turned serious once more. 'Find the girls and find Reaghan. Does your man know where he is now?'

'That's the rest of my news and I'm afraid it isn't good. When he reported to me last, Reaghan had headed into the Senator's home.'

'Bring that son of a bitch to me Dorran and you are welcome to tie him to a roasting pole if you see the need.' The Chieftain's eyes raged. 'But whatever you do, don't let Culaan get word of this. I need to deal with Reaghan in my own way and I don't want to have to punish my other son in the process.'

'I don't envy you in this Owyn. Culaan should have always been named heir. We all know it. Whatever possessed you to name Reaghan?'

'His mother. She was a witch Dorran, of that I am sure.'

Chapter 20

'You want me to help you find two whores and you won't tell me why?' Dorran only nodded and smiled at Morrigan's question.

'I will find out what you are up to you know. I always do.' Dorran nodded again as Morrigan rose from the table.

She rummaged through jars and wooden canisters, collecting herbs and implements as she went. The Druid dragged a stool over to the hearth, climbed upon it and reached up high, removing a stone to reveal a hollow.

'A nice little hiding hole.' Dorran remarked as he watched the old woman balance expertly on the small stool. 'You know you should be less agile for your age. You will reveal yourself to the wrong person one day.'

Morrigan turned around as she replaced the stone. 'You just forget you ever saw this hiding place Dorran and you are sworn to secrecy on all accounts you know. I will curse you otherwise.'

'No need for threats woman, your secret is safe with me.' Dorran continued to smile good-naturedly.

'I will need something from both the women. What do you have?'

'I'm not new to this Morrigan. It took some getting, but this is Meredith's hair brush.' Dorran revealed a bone-handled brush from his left pocket. 'I couldn't find anything of Deidre's, no one even knows where she lives when she isn't working. Let's hope they are together.'

Dorran handed the brush over to the Druid as she cleared the table. She reached for Dorran's cup, 'Wait up, I'm not finished yet.' He smiled as he emptied his drink. 'You know how much I love your tisane.'

'Oh stop it you old flirt. Just pass me the brush.' Morrigan pulled a small collection of hairs clear of the bristles and tossed them into a wooden bowl. She used a blade to shave shards from a fragrance bark as Dorran sniffed in the armour.

'That stuff always clears my nostrils.' Morrigan ignored the remark and continued. Two petals of yellow dandelion, four sprigs of jasmine and a handful of other herbs Dorran didn't recognised were added to the bowl.

'Is this really necessary? Can't you just click your fingers or something? Ariela can summon magic to her hands, why can't you?' Dorran teased. Morrigan only scowled at him.

'Mind your business Dorran. Don't try to understand what you were never meant to know. You shouldn't even be here while I do this.'

'But you love the attention, just admit it.' Morrigan smiled despite herself. 'You are lucky you are happily married now. Otherwise I would take you and make you forget your own name. You know I can.' Dorran only chuckled knowingly.

'Now be quiet. I have work to do.' Morrigan took a long sliver of wood and walked over the hearth. She placed the piece of wood into the smouldering coals and waited. The flames ignited the end and she gently blew on it to coax it to life as she made her way back to the table. She dropped the flaming shard into the bowl, the ingredients burst into flames, erupting with steam as though a kettle had been boiling.

The Druid lent over the fog and breathed it deep into her lungs before sitting down heavily on the bench next to the clansman. Dorran stood up behind her anxiously, ready to catch the old woman should she fall.

Morrigan's world swam as images flashed before her eyes and her stomach threatened to empty its contents from the motion sickness such visions often caused.

'She is frightened. I can feel her pain. She is hiding from the Romans. She is hiding from us all.'

Dorran resisted the urge to ask questions. He knew better than to speak and he refrained from touching Morrigan, even when she swayed.

'She is surrounded by hay. I can hear animals. Her body is hurting, her mind broken.' Morrigan swayed a little more before placing her hands on the table. 'I know where she is. No man will be able to touch her. I must go with you.'

Morrigan opened her eyes as she spoke the final words. Her mind was clear once more as she pushed herself upright. 'We don't have much time though, she is being hunted. We will need Genevieve and Culaan.'

'No, not Culaan, I promised Owyn.'

'What aren't you telling me?' Morrigan put her hands on her hips, her eyes boring into Dorran's very soul.

'Nothing you won't discover once we find the girl, but Owyn needs to make arrangements first, before Culaan finds out.'

Morrigan waited for more information, but nothing came. Dorran was fiercely loyal to Owyn and there was no way the Druid was going to get more from him unless he volunteered it. 'Very well. But we need Genevieve. She is the best tracker we have. I think Ariela can keep Culaan busy for now.' Dorran smiled his understanding.

'She is a fine woman. He could do worse.'

'He couldn't do much better but where Ariela goes, he may not wish to follow.' Dorran frowned but Morrigan was already past him and out the cabin door.

'As much as I hate horses, I think we will have to ride again Dorran.'

'Aye! I think you simply enjoy the feeling of my warm body against yours.' Dorran slapped the Druid on the backside as she left the room.

'Your lack of reverence for my position could come back to bite you yet clansman. You best be careful.' But there was no malice in her words.

Chapter 21

Ariela drew back the bow and released her breath slowly. As her lungs emptied, she loosened the shaft which thud home, right in the centre of the painted target.

'Well, now that is impressive. I think that might be better than you can manage Genie. What do you think?' Culaan almost looked proud, as though the shot were his own.

'Close. Let's see, shall we?' Genevieve drew her bow, resting her hand gently on her cheek as she took aim. The bolt left her bow cleanly and Ariela's arrow burst into pieces as Genevieve's arrow found its mark.

'My father would be impressed.' Ariela clapped her hands together. 'That was a remarkable shot. Truly.' She smiled at her new friend affectionately.

'Amazing! That was perfect.' Culaan slapped his thighs with excitement. 'You are both unnaturally gifted. Honestly.'

The small group was still laughing and hooting when Morrigan approached. 'Genevieve, do you mind if I borrow a moment of your time?'

Culaan looked from the Druid to his friend and back, his brow furrowed as Genevieve shrugged. 'Of course Morrigan, what can I do for you?'

'I have a favour to ask. Dorran here needs a tracker. Would you mind helping him?' Genevieve looked to Culaan who put down his bow and made to remove his quiver strap. 'Just Genevieve Culaan, you carry on with Ariela. I'm sure she can teach you a thing or two.'

Culaan was about to protest when Ariela released another arrow, the sound grabbing his attention. Culaan was once again focussed on the Priestess and spoke without taking his eyes from her.

'Are you alright with that Genevieve? It sounds like it's pretty straight forward, unless you want me to come along?' The Huntress looked from Ariela to her friend and hesitated a moment.

She stared at the Priestess's golden legs in the short tunic she wore and her full and rounded chest and understood the attraction. Ariela was gorgeous.

'I'll be fine. It won't take long will it Morrigan?'

'Not at all. We will return by nightfall. Isn't that right Dorran?' Everyone was nodding far too much and Genevieve noticed the awkward behaviour but Culaan seemed content to watch Ariela as she drew another shaft from her quiver.

'See you later.' Culaan waved without looking back. 'Let's test you with a sword since you seem to have outdone me with that bow.'

Ariela smiled her reply and Genevieve tried desperately to keep the disappointment from her eyes.

Morrigan patted her on the back as they walked away. 'Alright Wise One.' Genevieve adopted Dorran's affectionate name for the Druid knowing it would get her attention. 'You might have lover boy over there fooled,' she pointed her thumb at Culaan's back 'but you aren't fooling me. What is going on?'

'I'll explain on the way.'

'It's dangerous, isn't it?'

'It might be, but we can't bring Culaan into this, not yet.'

'Reaghan, it has to have something to do with him or Owyn.'

'You are too smart for your own good Genevieve.' Dorran spoke quietly and Morrigan questioned him with her eyes.

'I should have known.' Morrigan spoke when Dorran didn't meet her gaze. 'Let's get going. Dorran has a spare horse for you Huntress.'

'Oh fabulous! Another numb buttock coming my way.'

'You should get some more meat on that butt of yours and riding wouldn't hurt so much.' Dorran teased.

****

Genevieve was tired and hungry but she wanted to be sure she had the right place. She followed the barefoot tracks and studied the terrain carefully before quietly making her way back through the undergrowth.

'She's in there. I'm sure of it. When you mentioned cattle, I knew she had to be near old Shemus' barn.'

'I guessed as much too lass. He is the only mad man around here who insists on keeping his cattle indoors.'

'How many soldiers?' Dorran regained their focus as he peered over the low shrubs and squinted to see more in the deepening darkness.

'I'm not sure, four possibly five. The tracks were hard to read in the fading light.'

A scream pierced their discussions and carried easily in the still dusk air. Genevieve notched an arrow to her bow. Dorran put his hand on her arm. 'She's a whore. They won't hurt her.'

'Doesn't sound like she believes you. I'll not listen to that and neither should you.' Dorran cursed at the sound of the young woman crying as the soldiers took turns.

'She's right Dorran. The girl was frightened, not for her modesty, for her life. If we let them finish, they may very well kill her.' Morrigan urged the old soldier forward.

'Let's set a little fire under their belts.' Genevieve smiled as she drew flint from her pocket and packed her arrow head with tar and crushed dry chaff. 'Dorran, get ready to go in the rear of the barn.' The old man nodded and circled out around the building, understanding what the Huntress planned.

Genevieve waited until Dorran had made his way around the clearing. She struck the flint on a hard stone, the arrow placed perfectly to catch instantly.

She blew gently on the flame before notching the arrow and sending it flying gracefully through the air and into the open barn door. It was only moments before the soldiers came running out with flames licking at their boots. They were only silhouettes against the fired barn but Genevieve took practised aim. The first assailant fell with an arrow to the eye, the second drew his short sword while trying to do up the belt of his kilt, dropping both to the ground as an arrow pierced his groin.

'Was that really necessary?' Morrigan asked as she moved from her hiding place toward the barn.

'No, but certainly worth it.' Genevieve smiled as she released another two arrows, both finding their mark.

Both women moved hastily toward the barn before Genevieve grabbed Morrigan by the arm as another soldier appeared dragging Meredith by the throat. The girl cried hysterically, howling and clawing like a cornered wolf.

Genevieve drew her bow but struggled to get a clear shot in the poor light. 'Duck you silly girl.' She spoke softly knowing her words couldn't be heard.

'Put down the bow or the girl dies.' The soldier threatened until his eyes grew wide and the hand that held the terrified girl's throat loosened. Meredith ran, tripping over in the dirt as she frantically looked for safety. Morrigan watched Dorran pull his short-bladed knife clear of the soldiers back and wipe it on the man's tunic before sheathing it.

'Meredith, stay calm. You are safe.' Morrigan moved warily toward the girl who still lay sprawled on the ground where she had fallen. The Druid waited for Meredith to make eye contact, but she was so frightened she continued to claw at the dirt in panic, struggling to rise.

Genevieve slung her bow over her shoulder and ran to join Morrigan. 'It's alright Meredith. Morrigan is a healer, let her tend your wounds.' Genevieve begged the girl, moving closer as her wild eyes began to focus. The fight left her as she collapsed into Genevieve's arms, covered in dirt and grime looking like a feral animal.

Genevieve growled under her breath as her eyes took in the wounds on the poor girl. 'By the goddess Morrigan. Men can be such monsters.'

Dorran turned from the scene, shame filling his heart as tears filled his eyes. He made his way to the horses to ready them for travel.

Morrigan reached for the girl, hand outstretched as though she were approaching a rabid dog. The girl's body shook with suppressed sobs and as the Druid woman placed her hands on her, she let the first flow of tears free like the broken banks of a river.

Genevieve took a deep breath to gain control of her emotions. She watched the courage of the Druid closely and marvelled at her.

'Let's get you warm now lass.' Morrigan nodded to Dorran who brought the horses forward, never uttering a word, tears visible on his cheeks.

Chapter 22

Reaghan waited in shackles, impatiently scuffing his feet in the dirt floor of the hall and avoiding eye contact with any of his kin.

'I will hand the proceedings over to Morrigan.' Owyn spoke to the assembled counsel, addressing each one with a nod. 'As the Druid of our clan, Morrigan holds the power to pass judgement over such matters. I can't possibly be considered impartial in this moment.'

Morrigan frowned her concern to the Chieftain and brushed her robes into place as she stood and took her place on the raised wooden platform.

'Members of the Counsel. You are all aware of recent events including Ariela's imprisonment, the death of two local working girls and the apprehension of Reaghan. We have had him under watch for days and it is time we gave the Heir of our Clan the chance to share his own account of his actions.'

'What for! You have already made up your mind you old….' Reaghan's seething words were cut short as Dorran's elbow struck his lip. He lifted his shackled hands and patted the blood with his fingers before staring at his hands once more.

Dorran smiled and nodded for Morrigan to continue. 'As I was saying. Reaghan has the chance to share his side of events and I will interpret the truth of his words.' Morrigan held her hand out inviting Reaghan to speak. The eyes of the assembled counsel fell on the Chieftain's son and he shuddered under their gaze.

Reaghan looked into the crowd of people, his eyes resting on the whore who would bear witness against him. His gaze moved to Culaan whose face was impossible to read. The young man cleared his throat nervously. 'I, I don't know where to begin.'

Images flashed before his eyes and their contents surprised even him. The dead whore, the meeting with the Senator. He rung his hands together considering his words carefully.

'Just tell the truth Laddie. Believe it or not, the Druid will know if you speak falsely.' Dorran's menacing tone rattled the young clansman.

'I made a mistake.' Dorran choked on Reaghan's understatement. 'I made a few mistakes to be honest. I have a problem with women and Dominic, the Roman Commander exploited my lack of control.'

Reaghan finally made eye contact with his father, pleading for guidance or any kind of support. Owyn dropped his head and Reaghan visibly stiffened. 'I killed the whore by accident. Dominic said he would have me imprisoned unless I did him a favour. That favour was to give up the Israelite girl. Where was the harm, she is not our kin.'

'She was under our protection.' Culaan moved forward, barely containing his anger. He was met with Dorran's blade tapping gently on his chest.

'Calm yourself man. This is an official proceeding. Let your father do this the right way.'

'The right way would have been to kill the sick little bastard the first time he hurt a woman.' Culaan snarled but knew better than to raise his voice or challenge Dorran. The man was as big as an ox.

'She is a witch.' Reaghan begged his half-brother to support him. 'You saw what she did to my weapon by the waterfall.'

'You attacked her while she swam. She was without a weapon until she took yours.'

'Yes, but it's how she took it that really matters. I was protecting the Clan by handing her over to the authorities.'

'You lie to yourself and it dishonours us all. You wanted to hand her over because she overpowered you, shamed you.' Culaan held his temper barely in check. His father's voice broke into his rage and the warrior turned his eyes from Reaghan.

'*We* are the authorities Reaghan. That's where you seem to have this all so wrong.' Owyn stood as his words raged. 'We do not choose to be subservient to the Roman Empire. They *force* our obedience. Ariela was offered protection by the Druid Morrigan. Your brother came for her to protect her. You can't remain ignorant. You had no right to give her to the Romans.'

Morrigan raised her hands for silence but the room had erupted into shouts and confusion. The humming sound first began in her throat, then vibrated from the walls of the Chieftain's hall, growing louder and stronger with each passing moment.

The onlookers gasped as bright light began to emanate from the Druid's hands and swirls of gold and red made trails like a comet in the sky. Morrigan's lanky grey hair began to shine like silver thread and curls sprang up around her face. The lines around her eyes receded as her pupils sparkled like purple gemstones.

Ariela took a sudden breath as the raw energy rolled over her like a sandstorm and her power responded in kind. Her hair glowed with golden light and her fingers produced orbs of green. *'I told you I would be here when you needed me'*. Raziel's words hummed in her mind.

'We have more to worry about than Reaghan right now.' Owyn gaped at the Druid, his mouth wide open. 'The Romans are coming Owyn.' Morrigan moved with uncharacteristic speed toward the entrance as she spoke.

The Chieftain did not need to question the Druid. His men were on their feet and Dorran was already dragging Reaghan from the hall. 'Dorran, leave him. Tie him up somewhere. Gather the men.'

'There is no time Owyn. This fight is for those with the power of the gods. Ariela, Culaan, Genevieve, to me now.' Morrigan's voice sounded years younger and her authority rang throughout the hall.

Culaan looked at Ariela and resisted the temptation to touch her. She still glowed like the sun had risen directly behind her.

'I don't understand Morrigan.' Culaan raised an eyebrow and looked at Genie for answers. The Huntress shrugged her shoulders in reply as Ariela reached out to touch them both, pulling them to her with little effort.

The surge of power released from their union almost knocked them all from their feet and at first, the shock wave appeared to ignite the banner above their heads, until more arrows began to rain down inside the hall, sparking fires in all directions.

'Get out everyone, get out now.' Morrigan screamed 'The Romans know we have Reaghan. They know Ariela is here.'

Chapter 23

The Senator held the parchment in his hands. 'The Emperor wants all the Druids gone. No wielders of magic are to leave this place today. Do you understand *Commander*?'

The Commander looked at the red and gold insignia on his chest that marked his new rank, then transferred his nervous gaze to his men who seemed to mirror his anxiety. 'I'll do my best Sir.'

'You will do better than that boy. The Emperor was very clear. Magic or even the illusion of magic threatens the prosperity of Rome and we all know how much Rome loves her gold.'

'You heard the Senator men. Fire the hall.' The new Commander nudged his mount forward, sword raised to spear the head of the legion forward as flaming arrows sailed overhead.

As they entered the perimeter of the village, they were met with little or no resistance. The people had fled, there were no fighting men to stand against them and all the Commander could see was a small line of civilians standing outside the inferno that marked the place where once stood the Chieftain's hall.

'This is going to be easier than taking honey from a baby.' One soldier spoke confidently as the Commander continued to survey the undergrowth either side of the clearing with suspicion.

'The Gauls have never been known for coming quietly or giving up on a fight easily man. I wouldn't count your silver just yet.' The Commander spoke without taking his eyes from the small group who stood defiantly ahead.

****

'I told you to take Reaghan and get out of here Dorran.' Owyn glared at his lifelong friend.

'Yes you did. But when have I ever obeyed orders.?'

'Neither of you should be here.' Morrigan scowled. 'I told you, unless the gods have suddenly bestowed immortality on you while I wasn't looking, you should be far from here, heading to join the Trocmi clan by now.'

'I have sent word. They know that if we fall, the Romans will be on their way to Gordium next.'

'*If*, I love your optimism. Four warriors and two Druids against what, three hundred?' Genevieve laughed without humour and wiped her sweating palm on her tunic before casually pulling her thin leather gloves onto each hand.

'Don't underestimate our allies Genevieve.' Ariela spoke confidently and the young Huntress looked to Culaan for understanding. Ariela saw the exchange and smiled. 'I didn't travel thousands of miles and seven hundred years to lose.'

'Draw your weapons.' Morrigan ordered as the Roman Calvary rode into sight.

Culaan touched Ariela's arm gently, the now familiar buzz of energy tickled his finger tips and he smiled at the sensation while Ariela looked down at her arm in confusion. 'In case we don't make it.' Ariela made to speak but Culaan drew her into his arms and kissed her into silence.

'Draw your weapon you idiot. There will be time for that later.' Genevieve elbowed her friend in the ribs as she pulled her bow over her head. The weapon sung in her hands like it had never done before and as the Huntress drew an arrow from her quiver it began to glow in her hands like shining silver.

The white light pulsed but as she notched the arrow and drew on the bow the whole weapon vibrated and began to glow as bright as moonlight.

Culaan frowned at Genie's dig in his ribs but released Ariela when he saw his friend's face light up with excitement and the glow that now emanated from her weapon. She winked, 'Try your sword. I don't know about the gods or immortality, but I can tell you now, this weapon has never felt this good.'

Ariela tried to compose herself as she focused on the horses bearing down on them at speed.

Culaan raised his hand to his shoulder and fingered the hilt of his broadsword. 'All I can say is I am glad they decided to attack on our home soil so I could bring this to bear.' Culaan drew his weapon and as it

cleared the sheath it began to glow with purple and silver
light. 'What is going on Ariela?'

The young Priestess was still blushing from
Culaan's unexpected show of affection, but managed to
collect herself. 'The Angel Raziel has bestowed a gift
from God.'

'How do we use them?' Genevieve loosened an
arrow to test the weapon and gasped as the arrow head
burst into white fire on release. 'I think I could get used
to this.' She smiled and instantly released another shaft to
strike one of the men alongside the Roman Commander
as they charged their mounts forward.

The dust cloud rose as far as the eye could see and
Culaan turned to Genevieve. 'I hope you have an
unlimited supply of those things because that is one big
mob of soldiers coming our way.'

'Don't spoil the moment Culaan.' Genie drew
another arrow and fired again, this time the arrow
exploded behind the Commander sending riders flying
in all directions.

Ariela lifted her hands, waving them above her
head, fingers working as her lips moved soundlessly.
Swirling green balls of energy flew from her palms. 'This
is nothing like the power I have wielded back at Shiloh. I
hope I know what to do with it.' The power-charged
missiles landed amongst the galloping horses and both
men and beast flew into the air, amongst rocks and
debris.

The charge barely faltered. Dorran and Owyn
jumped forward and swung their heavy long swords
taking the closest horses' legs out from under them.

catapulting the riders into the air. The soldiers landed beyond the small group amongst the blazing fire and Dorran took a moment to turn and smile. 'That's fitting. Teach you flaming bastards to fire our village.'

Morrigan cringed at Dorran's language but refrained from speaking. She surveyed the group, the soldiers and her surroundings. 'We need to get to the Senator.'

'Yes.' Owyn agreed as he stabbed a downed Roman soldier and moved on to his next target. 'What do you have in mind?'

Morrigan smiled at the casual way the Chieftain discussed options as the white fire arrows flew from Genevieve's bow and Culaan's glowing sword seemed to spark with lightning taking down soldiers without ever touching them.

'Can you create a distraction?'

'Consider it done.' Owyn smiled mischievously at the Druid and returned his attention to the charging Cavalry.

'Ariela! With me!' Morrigan called as she moved away from the group, not stopping to look back.

The Priestess frowned but followed the Druid as she made her way around the outbuildings that surrounded the village hall. As they moved away from the fight, Ariela rushed to catch up with Morrigan. 'I don't like leaving them alone. They are new to their powers.'

'We have little choice Priestess. We need to get to the Senator if we have any hope of stopping the cavalry before they kill us all.'

Ariela nodded her understanding and Morrigan saw her look back to Culaan with concern. 'He will be fine lass. He has survived far more difficult times before you came along. If anyone can take care of himself Culaan can.'

Ariela blushed slightly as she dodged a rogue arrow.

Chapter 24

'There he is.' Morrigan pointed to a small group of soldiers in the clearing on the hill ahead. The Senator sat on his horse in the middle of the troop, his eyes scanning the battle below as he read maps and chatted casually with his Officers.

'What's your plan?' Ariela asked as her gazed followed Morrigan's.

'Follow my lead. We need him alive to stop his men and I'm not one for using my powers for murder.'

Ariela nodded her understanding as Morrigan moved up the hill using an outbuilding and a rocky outcrop for cover. They worked their way around behind the Senator and stepped into the clearing unseen. Ariela watched the Senator view the carnage below without passion.

The riders were so focussed on the fight, no one noticed the women until they were almost upon them.

The Senator jumped as something caught his eye and confusion erupted in the clearing as the women were finally recognised. 'Get the witches, now, before they get too close.' He backed his horse up, frantically trying to put distance between the women and himself. Fear rose in his belly and he fought to keep his stomach contents in place.

The soldiers looked from one to another, not quite understanding the danger two attractive and petite women could pose. Ariela smiled her sweetest smile and even made eye contact with the closest young soldier who returned the grin.

Morrigan spoke a few words in a language Ariela had never heard. Roots from below the ground began to wind upwards with great speed, taking a hold of the horses' legs and riveting them in place. The animals whinnied and threw their heads, but were kept statue still by their bindings.

The men began to call out to one another. Reaching for their swords they vaulted from there mounts to the ground, only to be swallowed up by more roots emerging from all around the clearing.

Ariela realised Morrigan was lost in a trance and unable to defend herself. Her eyes were glazed over as her hands waved in the air like a conductor at a grand event.

Two men cut their way clear of their organic restraints and sprinted towards the Priestess. Ariela raised her hands sending small star burst of light flying from her fingertips, knocking the two soldiers from their feet only to be met with more roots writhing over them until they disappeared below sprouting leaves and earth.

The Senator had managed to back his horse from the fray before his mount too became trapped. The movement of trees and dirt ceased as Morrigan's gaze cleared. Ariela saw the Senator running for the sanctuary of the surrounding forest.

'Hurry Ariela. If he makes it to the trees we will not find him in time to save the village.'

****

Owyn watched Morrigan leave with the young Priestess and looked at Dorran, a wicked smile on his lips. 'Now I understand how you managed to get yourself into trouble with the Druid.'

Dorran gazed past the Chieftain wistfully. 'My heart skipped a beat when she regained that form. Damned magic. I never did work out which body was the real one.'

'I am sure she has a few more options up her sleeve when she needs them.' Owyn nodded past Dorran, who turned his attention back to the mob of soldiers who were now on foot with shields locked into a tight formation.

'Damn the Roman strategist who came up with the fighting testudo. They will be harder to fight now than on horseback.'

Culaan moved alongside his father, noticing a small cut in the older man's arm. Owyn saw his gaze and smiled. 'You won't be rid of me that easy son.'

'It's not me who wants you gone.' Culaan answered as Genevieve joined him, frantically searched her surroundings.

'I need some high ground. I'll see if I can breech their defences.' The Huntress broke into a run and moved from the village square unhindered.

'She'll wreak havoc if she finds the right spot.' Culaan assured them.

'She could wreak havoc on any spot.' Dorran offered with a grin.

'You're old enough to be her grandfather old man.' Culaan smiled.

'Ah, but with old age comes great wisdom and I could teach her a thing or two.'

'No doubt, but your wife would cut your heart out,' Owyn reminded him 'and I like having you around old friend, so let's focus on these bastards eh?' The sound of precisely placed marching feet rang out and the clatter of shields brought everyone back to the present.

'Aye, point taken.' Dorran looked for Genevieve over his shoulder. She had climbed an old barn and sat in the loft, awaiting any opening she could find.

The Testudo moved forward in unison. Each man moved no further forward than his closest comrade and the soldiers' shields remained locked tightly together. The line behind held their shields aloft and covered their own heads and the head of the man in front of them. Another line did the same behind them. In total, the three warriors faced off against more than forty trained soldiers.

'Culaan looked at his magical sword with expectation and raised it before him.

'I wouldn't mind one of those.' Dorran offered.

'You will have to ask the Priestess.'

'Hmm. What favour do I need to offer to get one of those?'

'Not one I am not sure you can deliver on.'

'Stop it Dorran. Did you see any archers form up?' Owyn eyed the formation carefully.

'None. They are all swordsmen. The archers retreated with the Senator. I think they thought the battle won.'

'Well we best show them they were wrong.' Owyn swung his heavy broadsword above his head and moved forward, Dorran to his right, Culaan to his left.

****

Ariela ran over the mound of roots and soldiers before her, a hand reached for her ankle but missed as the Priestess jumped clear, narrowly missing a frenzied sword that appeared from beneath the matted roots. 'Senator, you have nowhere to run. You have seen our power. Stop and we guarantee your safety, run and the clansmen will not be so lenient.'

The Senator faltered for only a moment, just long enough for Ariela to close the space she needed. The Priestess spoke softly, 'now would be a great time for that help Raziel.'

'*Consider it done Priestess.*' The Angel's voice boomed into her mind. The Senator fell to his knees as a wind stronger than any storm threw him from his feet. Ariela turned toward the fierce hurricane and could see the ethereal energy of the angel Raziel with his wings beating almost invisibly, leaving streaks of silver in the air around him.

The wind ceased to throw leaves and branches across the clearing and Ariela turned to check on Morrigan who had taken shelter behind the wall of matted roots. The Senator was unconscious on the ground and Ariela moved cautiously toward him. The man groaned as she turned him over. 'It's nothing less than you deserve you know.'

There was no response. 'He would have no idea what you are talking about Priestess even if he were awake. Men like him know only power or lack of it. They don't understand eternal consequences.'

'How could he not see that attacking the village is barbaric?' Ariela tied the Senator's hands roughly as she spoke.

'You are talking about people who nail a man to a cross of wood to watch him slowly die of asphyxiation. You can't make them see that they are barbaric lass.'

My Uncle would see him beheaded.' Ariela dragged the Senator toward one of the horses that remained trapped in the bramble of vegetation. The animal's eyes were wild and it continued to fight its restraints.

'Be calm.' Ariela spoke softly, a gentle light flickering from her finger tips. 'That's it now, quietly, shoosh.' The horse flicked its ears and shook its head before neighing in resignation.

'Help me Morrigan, we need to get this pig up on the horse and threaten to cut his ugly head off his shoulders if his men don't stand down.'

Morrigan began to move the tree roots to do her bidding once more, but the horse threw its head in protest. The Druid moved forward to manually assist the Priestess to lift the Senator onto the still trapped horse. 'You know this body might look young, but it's still very old. Manual labour isn't easy at my age you know.'

Ariela laughed. 'Exactly how old are you anyway?'

Morrigan shrugged. 'I lost count too long ago.'

'I have a friend you would enjoying meeting. He can't recall exactly how old he is either.'

Morrigan raised an eyebrow. 'Really! Is he handsome?'

'He is too short for you Morrigan.'

'I don't know, I can be any height I wish you know.'

Ariela shook her head and continued to man-handle the Senator onto the horse. Once he was settled in place, she vaulted up behind him and Morrigan released the animal from the gnarled bonds.

Ariela trotted to allow the horse to calm down and then cantered through the clearing towards the outskirts of the village buildings. Morrigan freed another mount and cantered up behind her.

Chapter 25

The formation had moved steadily toward the warriors and now stopped some twenty paces beyond.

'They have to charge now. Without archers, they have no choice.' Culaan whispered to his father.

'You are sure there are only swords Dorran, no spears?'

'None that I saw.'

'Charge they must then.' As if on cue, the second and third line lifted their shield and began a closely formed charge.

Genevieve had the opening she had been waiting for. She notched an arrow that sprang to light and flew through the air, finding a target amongst the formation. The shields were raised too late and the charge faltered as the advance split in two.

Culaan moved first, his glowing sword causing soldiers in the rear to break and run.

'Oh it will be all over soon now lads.' Dorran chuckled and joined the fray. His sword crashed down on the first shield he saw. The young Roman soldiers stayed so close together, they could not swing their swords and with shields locked and their line holding, the Clansmen found only metal with each blow.

The sound of sword on shield rang out and even Culaan was beginning to tire. There had been no give in the shields and the Centurions were careful not to open their protective wall very often.

'They aim to wear us down.' He shared his fear.

'It seems to be their strategy.' Owyn agreed as another arrow found a rare mark amongst the shields. The Chieftain risked a look at Genevieve who smiled gleefully.

****

Reaghan watched from his hiding place. 'Stupid martyrs.' He mumbled to himself. 'Too busy trying to be heroes to notice what's really going on.' He smiled as he watched the two soldiers who had fled the battle earlier. They were both outside the barn where Genevieve hid, firing arrows into any unprotected man below. It was only a matter of time before they snuck in and killed her.

'It's a shame sweet Genevieve. I was hoping to take you for myself one day.' The Chieftain's son shrugged and slunk back into the undergrowth far away from any danger.

****

'Stop or your Senator dies.' Ariela's voiced sounded out above the ring of metal on metal.

The noise of fighting slowly resided as the Senator began to regain consciousness. He almost jumped as the cool metal of the Priestess's blade touched his neck. He began to squirm until Ariela pressed the blade a little harder and a trickle of blood ran down the Senator's tunic.

She rode forward without reigns, both legs gently edging the animal forward, one hand around the Senator's waist, the other holding the knife.

'You heard the girl. Stop!' The Senator pleaded. 'Now what?' He spoke to Ariela trying hard not to move the muscles of his throat.

'Now your men leave and I keep you alive. I will let you go when the village is totally clear of people and the Chieftain and his family are safe.'

'Why?' The Senator's tone was genuine.

'What do you mean why?' Ariela didn't take her eyes from the soldiers. They had lowered their shield from above, but had maintained their formation.

'Why save these people? They are not your people. Your people are allies of Rome.'

'I doubt they are willing allies of Rome. From what I have seen, Rome has no loyal allies. You suck the life out of all that you conquer and then when someone returns the favour, you seek to punish them.'

'You speak of my nephew and your punishment.'

'Of course I do. I was only defending myself. I am a stranger to this land and I was imprisoned and,' she hesitated to speak the truth, 'tortured and when I defended myself, you retaliated against me and everyone I know here. And you call the Gauls barbaric. What a jest!'

'You heard the lady. What will it be soldiers of Rome?' Owyn moved back from the shield wall, sheathing his sword and placing his hands on his hips.

'We say how much does the archer woman mean to you?' A voice came from the open loft doorway and all eyes turned to see a soldier holding Genevieve in much the same manner as Ariela held the Senator.

The Senator chuckled and loudly called to his man despite the blade at his throat. 'I knew you wouldn't let me down Commander.' His confidence beginning to return.

The soldier nodded from behind the Huntress, who appeared defeated, her shoulders sagging and her posture limp.

Culaan smiled. 'I've seen this ploy before.'

There was no time to explain. Ariela had not even begun to negotiate and her knife remained firmly against the Senators' exposed jugular.

Genevieve threw back her head, breaking the soldier's nose with an audible crack and knocking the knife from his hand before anyone had time to react. The second soldier ran at her as the first fell to his knees. Genevieve side stepped and pushed the already moving soldier over the edge of the loft. His arms and legs flailed in the air before he landed heavily on the hard-packed earth below.

Genevieve retrieved the knife from the hay-covered floor and slid the blade up under the soldier's armpit, past the edge of the chain mail and into the artery. She held him in an almost loving embrace until his legs gave way and she allowed his body to slide slowly to the ground.

The soldiers below were caught off guard but they rallied quickly, raising the swords once more and closing shields. Ariela took a sudden deep breath before speaking. 'Enough! The Senator will be spared, but only if you all leave this place now.'

The Roman soldiers stood still, swords half raised, their training ensuring they would not surrender without orders. They looked to the Senator and back to their fallen comrade. The swords moved in unison, the sound sending a chill into the air.

'You heard the Priestess men. Stand down. Return to town and await my return.'

There was only a moment of hesitation before the soldiers followed their orders. Dorran swung his sword menacingly in the air as the Roman battalion lowered their shields and began an organised march back to the Ankyra

'If I am not returned, they will be given new orders to attack again.'

'Even if you are returned the orders will be the same. Why should we let you go?' It was Owyn who answered the Senator as he moved to Ariela's horse and pulled the subdued man down to the ground.

'Because I gave my word.' Ariela interrupted, leaping gracefully down to join Owyn. 'Why hunt down those of faith Senator?' The Priestess returned her attention to the prisoner.

'Because the Emperor rules here and he doesn't like anyone holding any god or faith or power above him.'

Morrigan who had stayed back, giving Ariela the space to negotiate stepped forward, her hands on her hips and her face set grimly. 'Yes, and look where that has gotten him. He has made a martyr out of the Christian messiah and a new faith beats at his door. I have received letters from his Apostle begging us to spread the word of the new order. He and only he has embraced the miracle of magic. He claims such magic has raised his Lord from death.'

'Rumours, pure and utter gossip. It will never last. The Empire will not allow another religion to sully its power. The Judean leaders are happy, if they have money of course, and the Roman gods died out centuries ago. We have outgrown the notion of an almighty power. The only power that reigns on this earth is the power of Rome.

****

The soldier on duty nodded as Reaghan walked past him, entering the Senator's estate as though he lived there. The Clansman smiled confidently as he rolled a gold coin through his fingers and strolled into the grand entrance. He continued to fiddle with the coin as he ascended the stairs to the Senator's office.

Reaghan found the office unattended and instead of leaving, he chose to wander around the room, studying paintings and tapestries without genuine interest. His eyes fell on the side table where a jug of red wine stood accompanied by a copper tray of handcrafted clay goblets neatly displayed alongside.

The Clansman placed the coin in a concealed pocket and lifted a goblet from the tray. He poured himself a generous serve of wine, leaving space for water, but as he lifted the water jug he shook his head and placed it back on the table and proceeded to top up the goblet with wine until it almost overflowed.

After taking a long drink, Reaghan found a comfortable chair in front of the Senator's desk, reclined back and placed his feet onto the desk, sliding a pile of scrolls off onto the floor without concern.

'You took your time.' He greeted the Senator who wearily made his way into the room.

'What are you doing here Reaghan? I don't want to see your face right now.'

Reaghan frowned. This wasn't the welcome he had expected and he tried to stay calm, sensing the Senator was less than overjoyed. 'I've come to celebrate and to accept my title and my gold of course.' He kept his voice light and his mood positive.

'Your father lives,' The Senator shoved the young man's feet from the desk, causing him to spill his wine, 'and there will be no title or gold for you Reaghan. I think it's time I put you out of my misery.'

Reaghan fought the panic rising as he took another gulp of wine and put his feet firmly on the floor, considering his options. The temptation to run was growing strong. 'I know where they will go.' He blurted out. His only hope was to remain useful to the Senator.

'Do you now! I don't think it takes a genius to figure that out. You really are a useless little pup.'

'No need for insults Senator. You would be surprised at the options available to Owyn. I don't think you have any idea how he thinks, but I do.' Reaghan smiled knowingly and relaxed. He had this under control, for now at least.

Chapter 26

Ariela poured a cup of cool water and took a long drink as she watched the Clansmen's discussion. Culaan entered the hall, Genevieve followed a step behind. The Priestess watched the Huntress as she walked with sure steps and a permanent gentle smile on her lips.

Culaan waved in her direction and held his hands up for the guard on the door to search him for weapons.

Genevieve pulled her quiver from her shoulder and made to place her bow carefully on the table to join all the weapons that had already been surrendered. A clansman stepped forward to take the bow from her hand which sparked a threatening glare from the Huntress whose warning didn't go unnoticed as the Clansman backed away, hands held up in surrender.

Culaan laughed at his friend and shook his head as he walked over to greet Ariela. She tried to ignore the flutter of butterflies in her belly.

'We can't be too sure you know. With Reaghan having been a spy, there is no telling how many others there might be and we can't afford an assassination attempt on anyone here.' Culaan nodded to the huddled warriors who were now beginning to raise their voices.

****

'It's time the Clansmen moved north Garyth, across the Black Sea. The Romans will not stop until the Druids are all dead.'

'That's your choice Owyn. Our people will stay. The Trocmi clan have no quarrel with the Romans and we have no Druids left in any case.' The red-haired Clansman took a handful of nuts from the table and threw them all into his mouth at once.

'They will place us all into the one lot, Garyth, Macklyn, tell him. The soldiers won't care which clan colours we wear.' Owyn begged the grey-haired man on his left who rubbed his chin as he considered their options.

'So, what you are saying is that because you chose to save Morrigan's life, we will all suffer.' Garyth pointed his finger accusingly at the Chieftain, while Morrigan resisted the urge to speak. Instead she accepted the pat on her arm from Dorran who smiled at her frustration.

'No Garyth, what Owyn is saying is that to preserve who we are, our clans and our heritage, we must save the Druids and move our people as far from the Roman Empire as we can.' Owyn nodded his agreement and allowed some of the tension in his neck to ease.

'The Tolistobgii clan have always preferred to run rather than fight Macklyn. You only prove my point.' Garyth goaded the bigger man.

'So now you want to fight? Is that what you are saying Garyth? You can't seem to make up your mind.' Morrigan joined the group unable to stay quiet any longer. Dorran smiled at her comment and Owyn stifled a chuckle.

'Don't twist my words Druid. You stay out of this. It's your fault the Romans are trying to kill us all.' Garyth's face was growing red as he blundered through the argument.

'The only reason we are here my old friend is because Morrigan and Ariela, used their power to save us.' Owyn waved his hand in the Priestess's direction.

'The Druids are healers Owyn. All these rumours obsessed with magic that doesn't exist only serve to fuel the motivation of the Roman Empire. Why do you subscribe to such nonsense? Did you see it for yourself?' Garyth huffed and crossed his arms defensively over his chest as if to end the argument.

A low humming noise began, causing everyone in the room to turn to seek out the source. Morrigan smiled knowingly and nodded her encouragement to the Priestess. Garyth's eyes grew wide as his gaze fell on the small ball of energy that slowly turned on Ariela's palm

'I'm here for one thing and one thing only.' Ariela spoke clearly as she approached, her words carrying across the hall as her actions interrupted the proceedings. She had sat back and watched them bicker long enough. 'Your goddess spoke to my God who sent the Angel Raziel along with me to do what we could to save the Druids and the magic that is at the heart of your people. Now we have saved Morrigan for now, but she will need to find all the Druids and they will need you, the clans to ensure their safety.'

'It's a shame it takes an outsider to state the obvious.' Dorran joined the discussion, a sombre look on his face.

Owyn turned to Garyth and read his mood carefully. 'It's your call my friend. We have come too far, survived too many generations of Roman occupation to give up now but if you say we should throw our culture, our beliefs away and embrace Rome, then we will send the Druids away without our support.'

The red-haired leader brushed his beard with his fingers and chewed his lower lip. He looked from Owyn to Macklyn with a frown so deep his eyebrows almost touched. His eyes fell on the Priestess once more and he shrugged unexpectedly. 'Oh, for the love of the goddess, you two always get the better of me. Bring the ale, send the word out, gather those who wish to join us. We leave in three days.'

Ariela moved away from the gathering, mixed feeling flowing through her. 'What are you thinking?' Culaan moved up alongside the Priestess and touched her arm gently.

Ariela placed her hand over Culaan's and took a deep breath. 'I honestly don't know, but I have a feeling I won't be here for much longer.'

Culaan's brow creased with his concern. 'Why would you leave?'

'Culaan, I don't want to leave, but the Angel will come for me and soon, I can feel it. I have finished what he sent me here to do — save the magic of the Galatian Gauls'

'We are not out of trouble yet. The people need to make their way to safety. They are bound to run into trouble along the way, trouble that they will need your help with.'

'Morrigan will gather the Druids. They will grow in number when they find out the clans have finally turned their back on Rome and seek to protect them.' Ariela caught sight of Genevieve from the corner of her eye and saw the concern on her face.

'Well if you go, I am coming with you.' Culaan pulled Ariela into an embrace and ran his hand through a loose curl that hung over her eye. She was stunned for a moment, her heart beating faster and the butterflies had returned.

'And wherever he goes, I go too.' Genevieve leant over Culaan's shoulder and grinned. 'Now put her down, you know where she has been.'

Culaan returned the grin without taking his eyes from the Priestess. 'Yes, I know exactly where she has been, I just don't know where she is going yet.'

'What if Raziel won't let you come?'

'Then he will have to explain himself to me.'

'And to me.' The Huntress grinned menacingly.

'I don't think Raziel is afraid of arrows.' Ariela giggled.

Culaan had not yet released his embrace and Genevieve had taken her cue, moving away to join the growing celebrations.

'No, I guess Raziel is afraid of nothing but from what you have explained about how you came here, I don't think he will take you anywhere without your permission.' Culaan pulled the Priestess closer, his warm breath tickling her lips. 'So, it's simple, don't agree unless we all go.' He whispered the last, his face moving ever closer.

'I can't put you in that position.' Ariela could feel the heat rising to her cheeks.

'You don't have a choice. You're not leaving my sight anytime soon.' Culaan brushed Ariela's lips softly, then pulled away slightly, awaiting her response.

Ariela wrapped her arms around his neck and pulled him back firmly. The warrior smiled through the kiss for a heartbeat before his emotions got the better of him and Ariela's tongue found his.

Chapter 27

Reaghan grinned at the Senator, returned his feet to the man's desk and took a long drink of his wine, emptying what remained in the goblet.

'I think you are going to have to offer more than your assurances Reaghan. You haven't been the most reliable spy of late.' The Senator stared at the clansman's feet but said nothing. Instead he went to his desk drawer and opened it. He peered inside for a moment, a frown on his face as he seemed to ponder a major decision.

'You look worried Senator. Honestly, I will deliver the Druid to you, just give me a day or so to investigate the details.'

The Senator reached into the drawer and seemed to search for something. 'Your father knows of your transgressions. I think you might have worn out your usefulness Reaghan.' The knife flew through the air with little effort before the clansman found himself staring at the weapon protruding from his chest.

'I, I don't understand. I can ….' The Senator moved to the clansman and gazed at his lifeless eyes for only a moment before turning to leave his office.

He walked out into the hall and down the passageway toward the top of the stair. 'Two centurions to me.' He called, leaning over the balustrade to make sure his orders were heard.

A small group of soldiers came running into the foyer, swords drawn and eyes alert. 'No rush, he's done. I just need a little help getting him out of my sight. Call someone to clean up the blood.'

The soldier in the lead grinned and nodded his affirmation. 'I never did like that one Sir.' A round of murmurs followed before they made their way up the staircase.

****

'At this rate, the Legion will arrive before we leave Garyth. We must leave now.' Owyn paced the hall while Garyth and Macklyn tried to remain calm.

'We can't leave any of our people behind Owyn.' Macklyn spoke quietly, trying to maintain some composure .

'The word was sent out, you know as well as I do that some will choose to stay.' Garyth offered his opinion, expecting a backlash but none came.

'True enough Garyth, but you sent the word out offering them three days. It's only been two. If we leave early we condemn them to certain death.' Macklyn begged Morrigan for aid with his eyes. She watched him from the long table in the middle of the hall, not wanting to interrupt the proceedings for now, she nodded her understanding but waited.

'If they stay, they are dead anyway.' Garyth spoke without any obvious concern.

'Not necessarily. There are those who have been sympathetic to the Romans for generations, they will be able to make their case.' Owyn rubbed his chin as he tried to justify an early exodus.

Morrigan had heard enough. She rose and walked purposefully toward the Chieftains. All three men turned to her as she joined them. 'I will meet them on the road, before they reach Ankyra. I can't say how long I can delay them for, but I am sure I can gain another day, probably more.'

'You can't hold them back on your own Morrigan.' Owyn left the small group huddled around a low table and took her hand in his.' He looked around the hall to make sure no one else was present. The hall was dark and empty even in the daylight.

'You are the last person on earth I would expect to be sorry to see me go Owyn'

Owyn bowed his head. 'That was all a long time ago Morrigan. I no longer hold you responsible for Culaan's mother.' The Clansman struggled to use the woman's name or make eye contact again with the Druid.

'Andraste made her own choice that is true, but you were right to think I played a hand in it. She was powerful, maybe too powerful.'

'What did you do Morrigan?' Owyn's eyes shot up accusingly.

'I did what had to be done Owyn. Andraste was not any ordinary Druid woman. There was something else about her that I never really understood but when I saw Culaan and Genevieve wield those weapons, realisation struck.'

'What are you saying?'

'I'm saying I need to stop the Legion which marches against us as we speak. You will take our people, all of them who will come, and you will head into the territories of Thracia, then on into Macedonia. I have friends there who will ensure your safety.'

'You must come with us Morrigan. We need you to find all the Druids and restore the order.' Macklyn joined the closed conversation, trying unsuccessfully not to eavesdrop..

'A new order is coming Macklyn but you are right we must find more Druids.'

A furore broke into the small meeting as a large man with red cheeks forced his way past the clansmen who stood watch outside the hall.

'Morrigan, you are a beautiful sight to behold. Where is the old hag you love so much?' The man wrapped his arms around the Druid and embraced her in an all too familiar bear hug.

'Tristen! By the goddess. Did you come alone?'

'Happy to see you too my dear. Always down to business.' The man grinned mischievously. 'To answer your question! I brought a few friends with me. I hear we have a final stand to make. At last! I hate sitting idly by waiting for those damned Romans to wipe us off the face of the earth.'

Culaan stormed into the hall, Genevieve and Ariela not far behind him. 'We came as soon as we heard.'

'Heard what?'

'That you need help holding the Legion at bay.' Culaan smiled at the confusion.

'Who told you?' Morrigan held her hands on her hips, her eyes questioning the three Chieftains present.

'It wasn't any of us, we haven't left here.' Garyth pleaded his innocence.

'Ariela saw them coming, as you must have Morrigan.' Culaan offered an explanation as Ariela took in the newcomer with the Druid robe and thick grey hair.

'Who is Ariela?' Tristen frowned at Morrigan.

'No time Tristen. Let's go! Culaan, Ariela, Genevieve. If you are so adamant to offer aid, I won't be shy in accepting. Owyn, see to the clans.' The Chieftain nodded his understanding and for a moment he wanted to say more. His eyes focussed on Culaan with a frown, but Morrigan shook her head gently.

****

The Legion rode in formation. The vanguard of cavalry, followed by the main body of foot soldiers and further cavalry at the rear. Ariela gasped at the sheer magnitude of the numbers. 'There are so many. How can we possibly fight them all?'

'We don't fight them all Ariela. We are here to distract them.'

'Aye lass. If it is Druids they want, it is Druids they will get.' Tristen grinned from ear to ear with obvious excitement.

'You seem a little too eager?' Ariela raised an eyebrow in question.

'This has been a long time coming girl.'

'Priestess or Ariela will do fine thank you.' Culaan chuckled and Genevieve snorted as Tristen blustered to find the right words in retaliation.

Culaan looked down the line of combatants. He couldn't help but share Ariela's sentiment. Twelve Druids, one Priestess and two warriors were little more than bees to swat against five thousand men, even with magic.

'Tell me you all do more than mix herbs and potions.' Culaan pleaded as he drew his sword that hummed with familiarity in his hands.

'Praise the goddess. That's one pretty sword there laddie.' Tristen complimented.

'Praise whomever you like Druid, just make sure you offer up a prayer while you're at it.' Genevieve pulled an arrow from her quiver and drew her bow as the bolt burst into white flames.

'Oh this is precious. I haven't seen weapons the likes of these since the times of Ortagion himself.' The Druid to Tristen's left and right nodded in agreement as they focussed on their individual tasks.

The road was narrow, forcing the Legion to reduce their ranks to three abreast. As the Cavalry Officer caught sight of the small band of warriors he slowed his line, signalling for all to slow behind him. He had no time to do more before a wall of flames exploded before him.

The horses reared, toppling soldiers to the ground amongst flailing hooves. The smoke grew thick within moments and the soldiers didn't see the arrows until it was too late.

There was nowhere to run. The sides of the road were encroached upon by almost sheer rock walls cut out by the Roman's when they forged the main thoroughfare years before.

The surrounding area was thick with forest and heavy undergrowth.

'That will only keep them for a short while. They will find a way around the fire and the trench. We need to move back to the next strike point.' Morrigan nodded to Culaan in agreement and the band of rebels moved back to their horses and mounted up without delay.

****

Ariela looked at Culaan and smiled as she warmed her hands over the small campfire. They were both covered in soot and dirt but he was still very handsome with his now unkempt beard and bright blue eyes.

'We will be home tomorrow morning. I hope they have managed to leave.' Culaan suddenly looked concerned.

'You know you should probably stay with your people Culaan. I would understand if you decide to.' Ariela moved to the warrior and touched his arm with concern.

Culaan thought about Ariela's words for only a moment before he shook his head. 'No. There is nothing for me here. With the clans moving out to seek refuge elsewhere much will change. Three clans will become one.'

'But with Reaghan named a spy, he won't be traveling with your father. Don't you think your father should have family with him?'

'Owyn and I have never been close. There was always something about me that he didn't warm to. Something to do with my mother but I never met her, so I have no idea what his issue was.'

Ariela moved closer, placing her hand on Culaan's knee and willing him to wrap her in his arms. 'I'm sorry.' They sat in silence for a time before Ariela spoke again.

'Then I hope Raziel has no objection to you joining me because it will be time to move on soon.'

'I told you, he either takes me or he fights me.' Culaan grinned

****

Dawn was almost breaking on an empty village, with smokeless chimneys and a silent Birch tree standing at attention in the village square as if in mourning.

'We can stop for only a few hours and then we must move on after the clans.' Morrigan spoke to anyone who was close by. 'Collect whatever provisions you can find that have been left behind.'

'I won't be leaving with you Morrigan.' Ariela spoke quietly once the Druids dispersed.

'I know lass. I'm surprised you stayed this long.'

'That makes two of us. You must have still needed my help or Raziel would have come for me by now.'

'When will you leave?'

Ariela shrugged. 'I honestly don't know. The Angel hasn't exactly been forthcoming and I only know I need to leave because I can feel it, somewhere in here.' The Priestess placed her hand to her chest.

'Genevieve and Culaan will join you?'

'If Raziel will let them.' Ariela looked hopeful.

'Where will you go?' Morrigan moved closer to the Priestess wanting to embrace her but unsure if she should.

'I don't know yet, but I know I won't be going home, of that I am sure.' Ariela looked close to tears and Morrigan could hold back no longer. She embraced the girl in a gentle hug and stroked her hair with genuine care and affection.

The Druids were rummaging through the home when both Morrigan and Ariela felt the shift in the air around them.

Culaan and Genevieve turned from the quiet conversation they had been having outside the Huntress's hut to see a sunrise too early to be real. They covered their eyes and walked toward the light.

The words were spoken into Ariela's mind, leaving onlookers unaware. *It is time Priestess.*

'I knew you wouldn't be far away Raziel.' Ariela smiled. 'Anyone would think your ears were burning.' The Priestess tried to lighten her mood.

'Not without me Ariela.' Culaan yelled across the village square, a hint of panic in his voice.

'Or me.' Genevieve agreed as they both started to run toward the light.

Where you go, no one can return Priestess. You know this!

'So do they.' Ariela watched her friends running to her. 'Please let them come.' She begged with a tear in her eye.

'You heard me Angel. Where she goes, so do I.'

The light flickered and for a moment, the silhouette of a man with large silver wings appeared but it disappeared as quickly as it arrived.

The Druids were drawn out into the village square by the noise but their vision was obscured by the extreme brightness.

As you ask child, so it will be. No one should have to travel through eternity alone. Ariela smiled as she released the breath she had been holding.

'The Angel has agreed.' Morrigan concluded.

'Could you hear him?' The Priestess looked openly shocked.

Morrigan shook her head. 'No, but I could see your relief. I must tell them something before they go.'

Culaan and Genevieve arrived as Morrigan spoke.

'Tell us what?' Genevieve asked as Culaan placed his arm protectively around Ariela.

'What did the Angel say?' Culaan begged impatiently.

'Culaan, focus. I need to tell you something.' Morrigan instructed.

The light surrounding them became unbearably bright and the heat generated caused sweat to appear on Culaan's brow.

'You and Genevieve....' Morrigan begun.

'Yes, we will look after each other. Wish Owyn luck when you see him and make sure you explain what happened. I don't think he will believe you.' Culaan almost danced with excitement.

A wind started to blow. 'Hold my hand.' Ariela yelled above the noise. 'Don't let go whatever you do.'

Genevieve moved in to hold the Priestess's hand and took Culaan's at the same time. Ariela collected up Culaan's hand and the trio made a circle as leaves flew around them in a spiral.

Morrigan screamed above the rising dusk and almost deafening noise. 'Your sister. Genevieve is your sister. Culaan, did you hear me?' Morrigan watched the trio disappear before her eyes as the light ceased to exist in the blink of an eye.

What Now?

If you enjoyed *Call of the Druids*, I would really love to hear from you. You can leave a review with your favourite e-book retailer or share your review on my Facebook page.

While you are waiting for the next instalment in *The Priestess Chronicles* series, why not download the first book in my complete first series absolutely free by visiting my website at www.atime2write.com.au

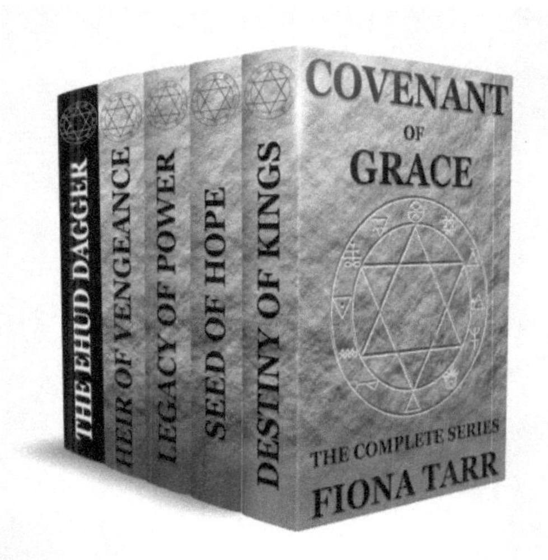

Dedication

This book is dedicated to all Indie authors who are yet to find their style. Just remember, it's always evolving, so keep writing.

Thanks to my beta team George and Rachel. Your feedback is always awesome. A special thanks to Kristen Fox of http://www.artoffoxvox.com for the Celtic symbol on the cover which my designer Simon masterfully crafted into what is probably my best cover to date; love your work both of you!

Books by Fiona Tarr

Covenant of Grace Series

Destiny of Kings
Seed of Hope
Legacy of Power
Heir of Vengeance
The Ehud Dagger Novella
Boxed set of the first 3 books
The Complete Collection – all 5 books

The Eternal Realm Series

The Jericho Prophecy

All books are available from your e-book retailer or online bookshop. You can follow me on Facebook, Instagram or my website at www.atime2write.com.au.

Thanks again for taking the time to read my work and I hope you get a chance to read more.

www.ingramcontent.com/pod-product-compliance
Lightning Source LLC
Chambersburg PA
CBHW020152120726

47903CB00007B/2520